TIME

CAROLE WESTWICK
With illustrator Bobby Dance

TIME TREE

For Lucas, Oliver, Tom, Cienna
and all the children I have known.

Acknowledgements and thanks to Lesley Rathkey for her editing; Judith Dunger for first drawing ideas; Guy Barlow for reading the book with his pupils; Ed, Will, Kate and Liz for their encouragement, James for his rendering, and to Maddie for being the first young person to read and critique.

Special thanks to Bobby Dance for his wonderful illustrations. Without him there would be no Time Tree book.

Carole Westwick

2022

TIME TREE

Children, it is true that even when things, bad things, fall from the sky it is still possible for adventures and magic to happen. It is still possible to listen to the whispered messages in the wind and find what is happening in other special places. Here is what happened to Stanley known as Stan, and his little brother Art (short for Arthur) who saw bad things fall from the sky and who escaped to the loving branches of a tree who had a special tale to tell.

RIDDLEME RIDDLEME RIDDLEME REE

CLIMB UP MY BRANCHES AND SEE WHAT I SEE.

RIDDLEME , RIDDLEME, RIDDLEME ROW

CLIMB UP MY BRANCHES AND KNOW WHAT I KNOW.

Contents

CHAPTER 1: STAN AND ART

Stan was 10 years old when he heard the word WAR and he knew it was a very bad thing. Stan lived in a street of small houses in somewhere called the East End of London. He knew war was horrible when he heard the screams of the sirens, the loud explosions of bombs falling from the sky and the thunder of guns trying to stop them. He knew war was terrible when the afternoon was full of the faraway humming of planes from somewhere called Germany. Then his mum would grab his hand and pick up Artie and run along the street and down the steps that led deep into the underground railway station near their house. Although deep underground, Stan thought it was like a castle and their protector against the deadly explosions and fires around them. Deep down below the street Stan and Art would cling close to Mum while she tried to find a space for them to sit on the crowded platform. Sometimes the heat and heavy stench of hundreds of people huddled together made Stan feel sick. Despite this, Stan dreaded the all clear siren sound because he knew they must leave the safety of their castle and climb back up the underground steps to the street. One day it didn't look like his street anymore. He stared at the house of their neighbour, Mrs Smith which was inside out; he could see her curtains billowing in the wind, her bath hanging over the floor edge; her bed was upside down and her sheets blowing like large white ghosts. Then he saw a black shoe like Mrs Smith wore, with a leg attached, all crooked, sticking out from under a pile of bricks.

Then his Mum said,

"Stanley don't look, just fix your eyes on our house; it's ok."

And on that day it was.

Art didn't know what war was. He was 6 years old and had said nothing much since his Dad had gone through the door because a letter had come to tell him he had to go. He saw his Dad wearing funny rough brown clothes and a strange triangle hat which didn't fit properly. He saw his Mum cry and Stan being told to be the man of the house and look after him. Then Dad went away and he hadn't seen him again. How Art missed his Dad; he missed helping him make things in the shed and riding in the side car of his motor bike. So Art didn't say much because there was nothing to say until he could shout, "Hello Dad," and be kissed by the rough top lip moustache once again. All Art knew was that the world had caught alight, the world was on fire and the noises made his ears ache; houses fell down and no one smiled or laughed anymore.

"I've forgot how to smile or laugh," said Art to his toy rabbit; " Expect Dad will show me how when he comes home."

Rabbit was a small knitted creature, made by Nanna for Art's dad when he was very small and now Art's best friend. Rabbit was brown with blue button eyes and the remains of a darned black nose and mouth. He wore a proud red waistcoat and bow tie. He had dear little paws which were good for sucking when you were sad or scared but tasted a bit odd. Without Rabbit Art knew he would forget how to breathe.

So Stanley was the man of the house and he took great care to look after Art and his mum. He knew his Dad was very brave and drove a big tank which would somehow stop the bombs landing on their street.

One good thing thought Stanley, his school had been closed. Mr Best, his teacher, had gone off to the Army like his dad. Some days Stan had to go for lessons in a house a few doors up with Miss Minty, an old lady who used to teach his mum. He had learned to read because he wanted to read his Dad's letters so he thought that he didn't really need to go to school anymore.

Then something really strange and terrible happened. Stan watched his Mum pack a small brown leather case with his and Art's clothes. She made him put on his school trousers and knitted grey pullover, his navy raincoat and his cap over his short sandy coloured hair. Art was dressed the same with the same mop of sandy hair which was longer than his brother's because he hated going to the barbers without his Dad. He had been to school only for a few weeks before it was closed because of the War and the danger of air raids. Art hadn't minded that much because he liked to be at home with his Mum and Rabbit. Mum made Stanley check that he was carrying his gasmask and Art's small gas mask case made to look like Mickey Mouse so it was not so scary. Stanley hated the rubber smell of the masks. He thought the smell must be worse than the invisible gas that he had been told could come in his street and poison them at any time.

When both boys were ready Mum took them to London St Pancras railway station. They stood in the big ticket hall where there were hundreds of children all looking like Stan and Art, especially with the same worried faces.

A lady came up to them. She had on the uniform of the Women's Voluntary Service with the initials WVS, sewn onto her coat. She carried a note pad and pen. She smiled in an official way and asked Mum to fill in a label with Stan's name on it and one for Art. The labels were tied onto their coats. The lady said to their Mum,

" Your boys are being evacuated on the next train. I will travel with them to a village in Hampshire. We will write to you with the address they will stay at. I am sure they will settle there and will be safe from the Blitz. You can write to them."

On the platform the three held hands and waited. Then Mum knelt down and hugged and kissed the boys and bit her lip so as not to cry. She told them,

"Stan, and Art, you are going on holiday; it will be lovely, with trees and fields and no bombs; you will be safe; you can go to school. Look after little Arthur for me, Stan. Dad will be proud of you; I will come to see you as soon as I can. Be good boys and do what you are told."

Then the roar of the large black steam engine came along to the platform. Stan held Art's hand tightly as he gulped in the smell of steam and coal. They were pushed into the carriage and jostled the other children to get to the window so they could wave goodbye to their mother. Art pressed his face to the door window and cried quietly as he watched his Mum wave and blow kisses. It was then he knew that the world had ended and he was going forever into a place where it was not safe to speak or smile. Stan squeezed Art's hand more tightly and said,

"Don't cry Art; I will look after you and Rabbit; we're on this big train, going on our hols; just us". Then Stan pulled Rabbit from his pocket as his mother had forgotten to pack him. Art held Rabbit's knitted body to his eyes and wiped his tears.

Stan and Art found places to sit on the long bench seat which ran between the carriage door and the window. Their backs were squashed against the carriage wall as other children pushed themselves onto the seat. No one said much as it seemed everyone was scared of this unknown destination. On the bench seat opposite to them, Stan noticed a girl was sitting and staring out of the window. She looked about 11 years old. She wore a blue coat with a velvet collar and had a blue ribbon tied in the side of her long, dark brown hair. She turned from the window and smiled at Stan and Art. Stan thought she had a kind face and hoped she would be put near them. The boy next to her was also well dressed, wearing a gray school uniform and cap with a coat of arms badge on the front. He too seemed about 11 yrs old. The boy suddenly stuck out his arm and tried to grab Rabbit.

"Give's it, the rag ball kid; it's full of fleas like you and your brother; I'll throw it out the window, do us all a big favour".

Art went pale and tightened his grip on Rabbit; still the large, rather grubby hand tugged at Rabbit's head. Then Art lowered his head and sunk his teeth into the hand. The boy screamed and let go.

"You little B..; I'll get you and your flea ball for that," he shouted.

"Serves you right, Freddy," said the kind faced girl, "He's only a kid; leave him alone or I'll tell".

"Bloomin' fine cousin you are," Freddy glared at her, "You're s'posed to be on my side."

"You forgotten Jack??" the girl said, "He was the same age as that boy and had a teddy he wouldn't let go of; you would've bashed anyone who tried to bully him".

Freddy's face crumpled as he remembered his little brother.

"Ruddy Germans got him and his bear," Freddy muttered as he sucked his sore hand while his cousin Alice squeezed his arm as a way of comforting him.

"That's why we're going somewhere really nice and safe, Fred. We'll get a good billet like Auntie Ethel said and we will be all tickety-boo, as they say".

Alice tried to cheer up her cousin who missed his little brother so much. Jack had been killed by falling masonry as he and his mother ran to the air raid shelter which had been built on the street. Freddy had run ahead to get there first. He had never forgiven himself for not taking Jack's hand and running with him. That was why he was nasty to Stan and Art because Art was still around and Jack wasn't. It wasn't fair.

Stan gazed at the kind girl and hoped even more that they would be near her. So he risked a smile and she smiled back.

"Thanks, I'm Stanley and this is my brother Artie; he's very scared. He shouldn't have bit your cousin but Rabbit is all he has of our home," said Stan staring into Alice's large blue eyes.

"I'm Alice and Freddy and me live with his mum, my Daddy's sister. My mum and dad are away, doing special war work and will win the war for us," Alice smiled back.

Then Stan knew why Alice had a posh blue coat and hair ribbon. Her mum and dad were working on secrets. They were probably spies and probably had tons of dough.

He gave Alice his best smile, usually saved for Mum after he had been bad. Art snuggled into Stan's shoulder, closed his eyes and fell asleep, first tucking Rabbit inside his coat.

Freddy looked at him and his eyes filled with tears. He was so like little Jack. Then he felt sad, angry and ashamed all at once and had to push Alice roughly to the side in order to feel better.

"It's ok, Fred," Alice whispered; "We're nearly there".

And Alice was right, they were nearly there; new homes, new school, new people and new adventures, if they just listened to the wind whispering to the branches of the woodland trees and heard the tales of the Tree who waited for them.

CHAPTER 2: EVACUEES

The train drew slowly into the small platform of the village station. Stanley looked out of the window and read the enamel station sign,

WELCOME TO BROCKEN END STATION

He stared at the flowers growing around the fence and the trees behind the station, so green and tall. So much colour he said to himself; where does all this colour come from? We don't have all this green and pink and blue at home he thought. He turned to Art.

"Wake up Artie, we're here".

Art opened his eyes slowly. Then he checked on Rabbit and smiled as Rabbit's ears tickled his chin from under his coat. Alice and Freddy stood up and moved to the corridor of the train. Alice turned back towards the boys and smiled.

"Come on", she said, "There's some people waiting for us".

Stanley took Art's hand and followed Alice along the corridor to the open train door. He and Art went down the steps slowly. Stan tried to be brave and stuck out his chin like his Father had told him to so as not to look scared. He saw two ladies and a man talking to the woman who had put them on the train. Then he saw that their case had been collected and put in a van;

"Hey", he shouted, " Leave that. That's ours".

"Don't worry Stanley," said the woman, "We're following your case to the Church Hall, just outside the station; then you'll find out about your new home".

"I don't want a new home," Stan muttered to himself, "I want my old one back".

Still holding Art's hand tightly, Stan followed the party of adults out through the station door and onto the pavement the outside. He could see Alice, Freddy and other children ahead of them. They turned right into a lane and then through a green door into a hall where chairs were put out and small tables with glasses of orange juice and small cakes. All the children sat at the tables as they were told and they were glad of the juice and cakes because they were hungry and thirsty after the journey.

The woman, Mrs Moore, then clapped her hands and told the children that the two ladies with her were now in charge. She introduced a tall, slim lady with greying hair, half covered by a brown felt beret which matched her brown coat. The lady spoke,

"Now children, I am Miss Brown from the W.V.S. I expect your mummies are in the one at home. We are in charge of finding kind people you can stay with. They will be here soon. We also baked the cakes for you so I hope you feel welcome at Brocken End. You will be safe here but must be good girls and boys. Sit still now until your people arrive."

Then Alice, who was nearby, whispered to Stanley, "Of course she is Miss Brown, brown all over".

Stanley smiled and again felt that Alice might be a sort of angel sent to look after them. Freddy grabbed the last cake on their plate but Art was too busy feeding crumbs to Rabbit to be bothered by him.

After a while the door to the hall opened and different grownups came in and collected brothers and sisters until only Stan and Art were left alongside Alice and Freddy. Miss Brown came to their table.

"Right Alice and Freddy you are billeted with me; just waiting for Nellie Winter to come for these two; she's always a bit late, almost certainly having car problems."

At that moment the door crashed open and there stood Nellie; she wore overalls and a bright red check shirt. She appeared to have oil on her hands and a bit on her face. She looked plump and kind and had a beaming smile.

"Are these my two, Mollie, skinny pair? We'll soon get them fattened up. Come on lads off to Auntie Nellie's car before she conks out again".

Stanley remembered the witch in Hansel and Gretel who tried to fatten up Hansel before she ate him. But Auntie Nellie was not witch like, so he took Art's hand and followed her slowly to her old car which was smoking and chugging outside. Auntie Nellie threw their case in the boot, sat them in the back and crashed the gears into first.

"Just up this hill and out towards the forest and you'll see my little cottage and my bit of land. So who's Art and who's Stan?" she asked.

Although he tried hard not to, Stan began to like his new Auntie. He replied,

"I am Stan and this is Art and oh, this is Rabbit, Art's best friend."

Stan hoped this would make Art feel better but Art stared at the top of Rabbit's head and tried hard to get out of this strange dream and back into his own little bed at home.

Soon the car turned into the path of a cottage. The cottage was really old Stan decided and noticed that it didn't have a real roof like his house in London, just some sort of grass stuffed under wire. The doorway was low and the two windows either side were dusty but Stan could see a fire glowing in a grate.

"Come on you two, into the house. This is your home for now and you are very welcome," said Auntie Nellie with a smile.

Auntie Nell collected the little case as Stan and Art got out of car and stood in front of the cottage. Then they heard the bark of a dog at the door and Art started to cry again and hid behind Stan.

"Don't worry," Auntie Nell said," It's only old Gwen, my dog; she loves boys and you'll love her."

Auntie Nell opened the door and a large, golden curly haired dog bounded up to them, tail wagging and mouth half open holding a ball. Gwen dropped the ball at Art's feet, looked him in the eyes and wagged her tail. Aunt Nell smiled and said gently,

"Art, Gwen wants you to throw the ball for her. She loves to play".

Art bent down slowly and carefully picked up the soggy, wet ball. He then threw it across the garden and Gwen bounded after it, picked it up in her mouth and ran back to the boys, dropping the ball at Art's feet again. Art stopped crying and thought that he liked Gwen.

"In you go" said Auntie Nell, " You can play with Gwen later".

The room was quite gloomy but warm and comfortable. There were big armchairs and a sofa in front of the fire and a big table at the back of the room, piled high with books and papers. Auntie Nell put down their case and showed them into the kitchen. Another fire was burning with a black stove over it and a kettle on the top which was whistling on the hearth.

"This is really old," said Stan, thinking of his history books at school.

"Yes it is old, it all belonged to my mother and Grandmother, who was a Victorian, but it all works and that's all that matters," laughed Auntie Nell.

Then Auntie made tea and gave them chicken soup from a pan that was on top of the old stove. She cut bread and buttered each slice. The boys sat at the long wooden kitchen table to eat their supper. Gwen crawled under the table and Art and Stan put their feet on her and rubbed her fur with their socks. (Shoes were off at the door, as their Mum had taught them). Art picked up his spoon and ate all his soup. Stan watched him, feeling relieved and ate his too.

After supper, Auntie Nell showed them their bedroom. They climbed up an old wooden staircase and along a landing with a wonky wooden floor and into a bedroom which overlooked the back garden. Two small beds were side by side, each had a colourful but faded patchwork quilt. The boys looked out through the small window. It was getting dark but they could see a big garden with trees and flowers, old buckets and best of all a chicken coop where they could hear the gentle clucking of hens.

"Tomorrow, Stan and Art, you have school but you can explore the garden after. It's lovely for making camps and climbing trees. I did that as a girl and had many adventures." mused Auntie Nell.

"Where's the lavvie?" asked Stan suddenly, looking around.

"Just outside the back door." laughed Auntie Nell, "There's a big pot under the bed, use that for now and I will bring you a jug of water to get washed."

Even our house has a lavatory inside thought Stan. This place is very old but still, perhaps fun he decided. The children got washed and put on their pyjamas. Stan and Art were tired now and snuggled into their little beds. Then Art sat up and cried out,

"Where's Rabbit?"

Auntie Nell looked around the bedroom. There sat Gwen with Rabbit in her mouth.

"Drop," said Auntie and Gwen obeyed. Art ran to Gwen and snatched up Rabbit. Then for the first time in a while he smiled and kissed Gwen's head. Gwen wagged her tail and lay down between the boys' beds.

"She can stay with you tonight," said their host quietly.

Both boys thanked her, put out their hands and stroked Gwen's long, soft fur as they went to sleep. Outside the trees whispered softly to them as they began to dream of home.

CHAPTER 3: SCHOOL

The boys woke up to see Auntie Nell drawing the curtains back to let the September sun come streaming into the bedroom. Gwen jumped onto Art's bed and licked his face as he woke up. Then she bounded across to Stan's bed and licked his hands and face.

"Well you've still got to wash, even though Gwen has made a good start." Said Auntie Nell and she poured hot water from a jug into two round white enamel wash bowls.

"Soap and towels just there," Auntie Nell pointed to the towels she had put next to the little bowls. "Come down to breakfast when you're dressed and have your porridge. There's lovely honey to put on it." Auntie Nellie left them to wash and dress.

Stan helped Art as he had seen his mother do. "I don't want to go to school, Stan; I want to go home," said Art in tears.

"It's ok Art; I'll be there with you and so will Rabbit. Put him under your jumper." said Stan.

The children climbed down the wooden stairs and into the kitchen where Auntie Nell had put a green checked cloth on the table and set out 2 bowls of creamy porridge. She helped the children put honey on their porridge and poured each of them a glass of milk. The food was delicious and Stan and Art enjoyed the breakfast.

"Now I am driving you down the hill to school, till you get used to the way." said Auntie Nell; "You will have lunch there and I will meet you at 3 o'clock to bring you home. Gwen will be here and ready for a good play with you. Your teachers are old friends of mine; be good boys for them."

Auntie Nell, Gwen and the boys climbed in the car. Auntie put her hands together and said the prayer which helped cars start and soon they were driving down the hill to school.

The school was next to the church, an old stone Victorian building with the word BOYS carved over one door and GIRLS carved over the other. Art and Stan walked through the gate slowly and stood in the playground with the other children who were running around and laughing. Stan recognised several brothers and sisters from the train. Then he spotted Alice and Freddy and waved to them. Alice waved back just as a grey-haired woman stepped into the playground and rang the big brass bell which she held in her hand.

"All children through the Boys' door today", she said. "New children from London go into the Hall and the rest of you to your usual classes."

Stan and Art held hands as they followed the group of London evacuees into the hall. Miss Simpkins put down the bell on a shelf and called their names from her register. When she called Stan's name she pointed him towards the junior class and then she called Art's name and pointed to the opposite infant class. Art held tightly to his brother's arm and started to cry.

"Please Miss," said Stan in a most polite voice. "Art has to stay with me. He's scared and I promised Mum I'd look after him."

"Nonsense, Stanley," said Miss Simpkins frowning; she had expected trouble from London boys but not this quickly.

"Arthur is a big boy now he is at school and he must come into my class." With that she took hold of Art's arm, ignored his tears and led him into the infant classroom. There Art was sat at a little round table with about ten other boys and girls.

Miss Simpkins looked at him and saw the bulky shape of Rabbit under his jumper.

"What's that you have there, Arthur?" said Miss Simpkins looking over her glasses. Art looked down. He wasn't sure what she meant because he wasn't used to hearing his full name. Miss Simpkins walked across to Art and pulled Rabbit's leg which was hanging from Art's pullover. "I'll keep this till you go home. We don't bring toys to school."

She put Rabbit on her desk.

Art went pink with anger and shouted, "He is not a toy. He is Rabbit and I have to look after him for my Dad; he's driving a big tank."

Some of the other children sniggered at this funny little boy and his tatty rabbit.

Miss Simpkins was not used to any child answering her back or shouting at her. Just as she thought these London children were trouble, hooligans who would be difficult to manage.

" Stand up, you rude boy," said Miss Simpkins in an icy voice. Then she took Art's chair and moved it to face a wall all on his own, away from the other children. "Sit there until you learn to behave".

Art sat staring at the wall whilst the other children were given puzzles to do and books to read; he looked at some of the pictures along the wall. There were angels flying above some fields and as he looked he decided he would learn to fly away from this horrible place.

Miss Simpkins rang the bell for play time.

"Stay there Arthur," she said, "No play for you at the moment".

As soon as she left the room Art jumped up from his seat and grabbed Rabbit from his Teacher's desk. Then he ran into the playground and across to where Stan was looking for him. Art saw the school gate and ran straight through and started up the hill. Stan was astonished and ran after Art, calling his name. Stan caught up with his brother and Rabbit towards the top of the hill where the path started into the Forest.

When they stopped for breath Art told Stan what had happened. "She's a witch. She's going to kill Rabbit; I have to get him away, safe! I hate school!"

"All right, Art let's go into the forest where we can hide while I think of something." Stan didn't know what to do and anyway he was in Alice's class with Miss Taylor who was nice.

The boys wandered into the green warmth of the forest and stopped under the branches of a very, very old oak tree. Its leaves were thick and green. It was so tall that its top could not be seen.

"Let's climb this tree, Art. No one can find us till I think what to do," said Stan.

They began to climb into the lower branches and the Tree seemed to stoop and lift them gently into its arms. They heard the breeze whispering through the leaves and Stan was sure there was a soft voice coming from the branches.

"Climb my branches and see what I see

Riddleme, riddleme, riddlemeree

Climb my branches and know what I know

Riddleme riddleme, riddlemerow.

And as if by magic the boys were pushed high into the Tree where they sat safely and comfortably in the strong, welcoming arms of the ancient Oak.

CHAPTER 4: A NOBLE CAUSE

It did seem very strange to Stanley and Art that they felt so safe, climbing the branches of the tree. Mum had always said tree climbing was dangerous and they must not do it. They had never climbed a tree before. Firstly, there were no trees in their street and secondly because of Mum's warning. But, Stanley thought to himself, this was a different tree. And Stanley was right. As the boys started to climb, the old oak tree appeared to wrap its branches and leaves around the boys, pushing them up until they found comfortable, flat spaces like seats on its high branches.

"We're safe here, Rabbit," Art whispered into the ear of his woolly toy.

"Yes," said Stan and he looked up to see just how far away the top of the tree would be to climb. The dense branches of brown and green blocked his view. Then to his astonishment he saw a shoe dangling just a few inches above his head, a strange looking black shoe with a square toe and silver buckle in the centre. He had never seen such a shoe before. Then he noticed that the shoe had a foot and black stockinged leg travelling up to the next branch. Then he noticed that the knee had buttoned trousers. At that point the man whose leg it was, slithered down to sit with the boys. Stanley stared at his brown, strong face and dark moustache. He had shoulder length hair and wore a long jacket which had gold braid and shiny buttons. Stanley thought he had seen pictures like this in his Beacon Readers History book.

Then the man put his finger to his lips and whispered,

"Shhh Boys!! Are they looking for you too?"

Art's eyes filled with tears as he remembered his horrible teacher. What if she was looking for him and Rabbit!!

"Yes," said Stan, " I think Auntie Nell will be very cross with us for running away from school. People may be out searching for us right now."

"School, School?" said the man, "Are you whipping boys? I had one, you know. Every time I disobeyed the Master he got beaten instead of me. The Royal flesh can't be touched you know or that was so before that dog, Cromwell stole my birth-right. Anyway my whipping boy became a Duke, can't remember of where. Don't know where he is now, perhaps running for his life, like me".

Stanley was alarmed. Was this a madman pretending to be the King?

The man continued, "Now tell me lads, before you climbed, did you see any soldiers around? Cromwell's Roundheads, are they marching this way? They're after me, the curs. My men and me, we landed too early."

Art looked up at the man. "My dad's a soldier. He hasn't got a round head. He has a brown cap and drives a tank. Mum says he could be in France."

The man looked shocked. "Then he may be one of ours. Who is he fighting?"

"Germans of course; don't you know nothing Mister?" said Art scornfully. "Wish he could come home so I could ride his motor bike again".

The boys and the man stared at each other, all totally confused by the strangeness of the conversation. Stanley began to remember some of his history lessons. He remembered Mr Best teaching them about King Charles I, who two hundred years earlier, had argued with the English Parliament and closed it down. Then the leader of Parliament, Oliver Cromwell got together an army, called Roundheads and fought lots of battles with the King's men, the Cavaliers. Cromwell and his army won and Charles I was beheaded in London. His family had escaped to France but his son had made several attempts to raise an army to win back his throne.

Stanley felt uncomfortable as he remembered this story but he looked at the man and said, "I am Stanley and this is my brother Art. Who are you?"

"I, sir, am Charles Stuart, rightful King of England, Wales, Scotland and Ireland, son of the most noble and brave King Charles I. Unfortunately, I am currently in hiding from my enemies. Pleased to make your acquaintance I am sure."

At that moment the sound of horses' hooves and marching feet could be heard; loudly they approached the Tree from the far side of the wood.

"Quiet now, boys" said the King. "They must not suspect we are hiding up here."

"Are they Germans?" whispered Art, feeling terrified.

"No, Cromwell's men," replied the King. "They fought against us at Worcester. We were beaten by these dogs. Betrayed by the Scots again who didn't send us the promised troops. I got away from the Battle in disguise. Now I am trying to get to the coast to get back to France".

"What year did you land Sir?" asked Stan carefully.

"This year," replied the King, "1651; we had the French with us but not enough of them to win".

Just then they heard some horses stop beneath the Tree and the voices of men rang up into the branches.

Stan looked at Art and whispered, "Me, you and Rabbit, Art. We're having an adventure".

The man put a gloved finger to his lips. "Shhh," he whispered, "The devils may take me and then you as well if they know you are Cavaliers".

" We ain't Cava-whatsits", replied Art, "We're Londoners".

"Sorry Sir," said Stanley, "about your father I mean. So cruel; such a wicked thing to do".

The man looked up in surprise. "Were you there lad, in the crowd that day around Whitehall? Did you see him? He died bravely and nobly like the best of kings. I tried to save him but couldn't get an army. One day these dogs will pay."

"They do Sir. I read about it."

"Good to know the pamphleteers are at work already, lad, telling his story. But they must not get me as my head will go the same way as my Father's. I must stay here till night and then go on foot to the coast where friends will meet me."

"Dad says never lose your head," whispered Art, "he says stay calm and carry on."

"Good form your Pa!" smiled the King. " I should like to meet the man one day. Has he his own musket and pistols for fighting?"

"He drives a tank," said Art.

Just then there was shouting from a Roundhead Captain from below the tree. "The Traitor's cursed son is here in the forest. He was seen at dawn climbing a tree. Get searching men. A bounty for whoever finds him."

Then a strange thing happened. The lower branches of the tree seemed to curl and shrivel and grow sharp thorns. The soldier looked up and ran his hand on the bottom thin branches. "Ouch". He said and sucked the blood from his cut where the thorns had scratched. "No one could get up there". Then he walked away to inspect other trees.

There were shouts from the Roundhead soldiers as they searched for the King. Eventually it began to get dark and the order was given for the soldiers to leave. The marching feet and trampling of hooves could be heard to get fainter as the troop left the area.

"I better leave now", said the man and made ready to slide down the branches.

"No Sir," said Stanley, "Art and me will go and see it's all clear for you. England needs you now and in a few years time you will be King again."

The man looked strangely shaken, "Quite so my little sorcerer. Royal thanks indeed."

Stanley and Art climbed slowly from branch to branch and jumped to the ground. The thorns had gone and the leaves were soft and strong. They looked around carefully and then called up to the man to come down to the ground.

The man appeared and looked handsome and young in the evening light, and exactly like a King, Stanley thought.

"Thank you my people". He said and bowed his head briefly. "I hope we meet again in London one day. Now I must run, not like a king but like a hunted stag. Farewell." And quickly he was gone into the shadows of the forest.

"Who was that geezer?" Art asked Stanley as they began to walk back down the path towards Auntie Nell's cottage. "He did talk funny."

"That was King Charles the Second," said Stanley, scarcely believing his own voice.

"Never heard of him. Neither has Rabbit. Do you mean Charlie Chaplin? I like his pictures and he is a Londoner like us."

Just then they heard Auntie Nell's voice calling them from the cottage. "Stan, Art, please come. Tea's ready. Nothing to worry about. We just want you home."

Then Gwen bounded up to Art, licked his face and tried to steal Rabbit. Auntie Nell hugged the two boys. "Come on. Eggs on toast for tea and you can tell me all your adventures while we eat."

Home they went to the little cottage, a roaring fire, toast, eggs and sweet tea.

Glad to be back in this century thought Stan to himself even with a war on.

CHAPTER 5: RABBIT IN THE BAG

As they ate their tea the children began to relax. Auntie Nell had made some little lemon cakes with white icing and initials drawn into them and these were on a pretty pink and green plate and smelled delicious. She smiled and looked at Art.

"Now, Art, please tell me if you and Rabbit have room for a little cake. Can you see A for Art and R for Rabbit on two of them?"

Art had decided that to speak might mean trouble so he buried his face in Rabbit's neck and said nothing although he longed for a little sweet cake like Mum had got from the baker's shop a long time ago.

"Rabbit, please squeak if you would like your cake," said the wise Auntie.

Art knew that Rabbit was hungry and loved sugar so with great courage he squeaked quite loudly and Auntie Nell clapped her hands and put Rabbit's cake on Art's plate. Then Stan laughed as he reached for the cake with the S.

"These are nice," said Stan, "Ta, err, thanks I mean. Art can you see your cake with the A on it?"

Art peeped out from where he was helping Rabbit to eat his cake and nodded.

"Would you like it?" said Auntie gently.

"Yes," whispered Art and Auntie Nell smiled with relief that the child had managed to speak. 'Please' could come later.

Then Auntie explained to the boys that she had driven down to the school a bit late because once again the car had refused to start. When she could not see the children she went in search of the teachers who described the boys as very difficult. Miss Simpkins spoke of Arthur's rude behaviour and explained that she had assumed the boys had gone home to her. Auntie Nell did not tell Art and Stan the difficult bit or how she had told the ladies concerned how unkind they were not to have more sympathy for a frightened 6 year old boy who needed his Rabbit for security. The teachers did look uncomfortable at this point but said rules were rules and that meant no toys in school. Since the teachers were rather worried about being in trouble with the Billeting Officer, an important man from the Church Council who was in charge of everything, they agreed that Rabbit could enter school in a bag which could be hung up with Art's coat on his peg.

Auntie Nell then produced a striped bag in yellow and gray with a drawstring through the opening. (It had once held her pegs but she had washed and ironed it and now it looked like new.)

She passed it across the table to Art and said, "Does Rabbit fit nicely into his new sleeping bag?"

Art wiped the crumbs from Rabbit's mouth and carefully put him in the bag.

"Jolly good. I love it." said Stan.

"And Rabbit loves it too," whispered Art and smiled a little.

Then Auntie Nell lay back in her chair and pretended to yawn before casually asking Stan where he and Art had spent the afternoon.

"Oh we were just in the forest where you found us, looking at the trees and trying to climb them. We got lost and sorry, we didn't mean to cause any trouble and bother".

Then Art looked up and decided after two cakes it was safe to speak.

"We met Charlie Chaplin, I think," said Art.

Stanley kicked Art's legs under the table. He hadn't expected his silent brother to start to speak about the adventure.

"Just a game we played Auntie Nell. You know Charles and the Roundheads hiding in the Forest," said Stan quickly.

Auntie Nell smiled again and seemed to be lost in thought.

"Yes I do know, my dears, I think I do know exactly". She said.

So after some fun with Gwen the dog in the garden and their first lesson in feeding the chickens, the children were tired.

In their bedroom the boys could hear the gentle clucking of the hens like a soft lullabye. Gwen added her low snores from the space between the boys' beds. So Stanley and Art were soothed by these soft sounds and slept well in their new beds. But still they dreamed of Roundheads and Germans.

The next day Art took Rabbit to school in the little sleeping bag and hung him on the coat peg with his jacket. Strangely Rabbit kept leaving his bag and somehow found his way to Art's pocket, quietly and secretly so no one knew.

Stan was happy playing with Alice in the yard at play time. Even Freddy was a little bit nicer and kicked a football which Miss Brown had found for him. And so the four children formed an odd but happier group. Stan kept thinking about the Tree and the strange man they had met, until he wasn't sure whether he had dreamed the whole thing, It was no good talking to Art about it; he seemed to think it was like a Charlie Chaplin film he had seen once. Stan wanted to tell Alice but was worried that she would think he was silly or a liar or both. But he should have known better for Alice was a special girl whose parents were working on decoding secret messages from brave agents and spies hidden in Europe. She was born to solve mysteries.

CHAPTER 6: CLIMBING HIGHER

The days were warm in that September 1940. Auntie Nell said the boys had been so good to settle into school that they could take a picnic into the forest and play on Saturday. Stanley took a chance, smiled his best smile and mentioned the two new friends living with Miss Brown.

Auntie Nell laughed and said she knew Molly Brown well and would ask her to bring Alice and Freddy to the picnic so long as they all stayed on the forest edge. For a moment Nellie looked sad and remembered her brother Frank who had become engaged to marry the lovely Molly Brown before volunteering for the Army as the First World War started. He was brave and respected and soon became Captain Frank Winter. Then she put the memory aside and didn't burden the children with the fate of the many brave young soldiers just twenty odd years earlier.

That Saturday morning Stanley combed his hair carefully and put some cold water on the sticking up bits. He put on a sleeveless jumper over his grey school shirt. This had a bright colourful diamond pattern and he thought Alice might like it. He had old patched shorts which he thought made him look like an adventurer. He pulled on his lace up plimsolls and looked at himself in the mirror. Auntie Nell watched him, smiled and said,

"Stan, you look so smart and ready for anything. I think Alice (and Freddy), of course, will be impressed."

Stanley blushed a little and bent low to pull up his socks so no one would see.

Meanwhile Art was sitting on the floor teasing Gwen with Rabbit. He hadn't bothered to think about clothes and had grabbed his old jumper and shorts but he was ready for the day's adventure.

At 11 0clock a smart car pulled up into the yard and Alice and Freddy jumped out. Alice walked to the door with Molly Brown. Alice was wearing a grey pinafore dress over a white shirt and a knitted lavender cardigan with flowers embroidered on it. She had long grey socks and brown laced up shoes. Stanley noticed the bow in her dark hair was lavender to match her cardigan. Miss Brown was so delighted to have this lovely girl to stay and couldn't resist adding some pretty bits to the bag of clothes she had brought. She thought to herself wistfully that Alice was the daughter she would have had if her fiancé Captain Frank Winter had survived the Battle of the Somme where he was killed in the First World War. How strange she mused to herself that the Second World War had given her the child the First war had stolen, at least for a while. Freddy was a different matter; an angry, scowling boy whom only Alice could soothe. Nevertheless the football had helped and she noticed he was already kicking it against the shed wall with some force.

Auntie Nell opened the top half of the stable style kitchen door to welcome her visitors, followed immediately by Gwen rushing out through the bottom section. Then disaster, Gwen made a dash for the football, caught it in her mouth as it bounced off the shed wall and ran around with her tail wagging. Art giggled, glad that Rabbit was no longer of interest to Gwen, but Stan and Alice held their breath expecting Freddy to lose his temper. Auntie Nellie and Molly Brown looked worried as they waited for Freddie to react. Much to everyone's surprise, Freddy laughed and called, "Here Gwen, fetch the ball. We can play". As if she knew Gwen dropped the ball at Freddy's feet. At first Freddy thought he might kick the dog to teach her a lesson but then he patted her head and said "Good dog, good girl". In that moment Freddy felt tears come to his eyes as once again he had a fleeting picture in his head of Jack lying on the pavement under debris. But as he stroked the dog's head, he felt better than he had for a long time. Even so, the ball was too precious to share with a dog with sharp teeth so Freddy threw some sticks for her which Auntie Nell kept by the door. Soon Freddy and Gwen understood each other and became best friends. Molly and Nell looked at each other,

"Thank goodness for dogs," said Molly.

"Thank goodness for footballs," said Auntie Nell

"And sticks," whispered Alice to Stan.

"And Rabbit," shouted Art holding him up for all to see.

"And Rabbit indeed," thought Auntie Nell , relieved that the child had spoken without looking as though the world might end if he opened his mouth to speak.

Auntie Nell gave Stan a brown canvas bag to carry on his back which contained some spam and cheese sandwiches, ginger biscuits she had made and some apples. Alice carried a little bag as well with some homemade lemonade and old china cups so they had a drink when they needed it.

"Now don't go too far into the Forest, children," said Nell, "Have fun, eat your picnic and Gwen and I will come for you in a few hours. Stay together and then you can't get lost."

Freddy picked up his football and called back to the two kindly ladies who were waving: "Don't worry, I will look after them." No one was more surprised to hear his words than Freddy himself and again he felt a bit better.

The four children went into the forest along the green path with brambles, wild flowers and trees on either side. They did not mean to go too far but they each could hear a whisper in the leaves above their heads urging them on. The flickering sunlight through the trees seemed to guide their path deeper into the Forest's secret places and, like a magnet, Stanley felt the pull of the old oak tree draw him closer.

And there it was, the majestic tree a few yards from the overgrown path, its branches gently swaying and singing to the children in the warm breeze:

Climb up my branches and see what I see
Climb up my branches and know what I know

Stanley left the path and ran to the tree. He placed his arms as if to hug the great trunk and put his face on the rough bark. Art ran after him but Alice stopped in her tracks and wondered about this odd behaviour. Freddy didn't wonder at all but placed his football on the ground and kicked it as hard as he could towards Stan thinking it would hit him on the back. He watched as the ball rose higher and higher and then seemed to get lost in the branches of the tree.

"Yikes", he shouted "Just look at that boot, I am so good!", and he went around the tree to see where the ball had landed but it was nowhere to be seen.

"Blast," Freddy muttered to himself realising that it must be caught in the high branches of the tree.

Stanley walked round with Freddy trying to help find the ball, without realising he had been the target of Freddy's malicious kick.

"Guess we'll have to climb the tree and look for it, Fred", smiled Stan.

"Yes", whispered Art to Rabbit, "We might see that man again who talked funny."

"What man, Art?" asked Alice.

"We will tell you later,"said Stan uncertainly, "But Alice can you climb in that skirt?"

"Watch me," shouted Alice as she swung up into the branches. She remembered her mother telling her before she left that girls could do anything boys could do and that was why she was an active officer in the War. But Alice need not have tried so hard because the Tree wrapped its soft branches around her legs and gently pushed her from branch to branch until she was safely on a large old branch towards the tree top.

Not to be outdone by a mere girl, Freddy rushed to the lower branches and followed Alice in her climb but seemed to find it quite hard as the tree offered him little help. Then Stanley pulled Art into the bottom branches and they too followed Alice higher and higher until they reached the large flat branches towards the tree top.

"He aint here, Stan, Charlie Chaplin," whispered Art to his brother.

"What an idiot," said Freddy poking Art, "Course he isn't; he lives in Hollywood".

"Well he was in **this** wood wasn't he Stan?" said Art, disliking Freddy even more.

Alice was trying to understand what was going on when she heard the sound of a horse riding towards them. Then silence except for the horse's chomping of grasses around the ferns of the path. The children froze as they heard someone else climbing the branches into the tree and as he climbed he groaned as if in pain.

"Shh," Stanley gestured to the others, putting a finger to his lips. "We may have trouble."

CHAPTER 7: YOUR MONEY OR YOUR LIFE!!

The children sat quietly, hardly daring to breathe as they listened to the cracking of twigs and the slow, painful breaths of the approaching figure. Then a black 3-cornered hat came close to Alice's shoulder. Under the hat was a pale, sallow face framed by black hair tied into a pony tail at the back of the neck. Small dark eyes half open, looked at Alice and the thin lipped mouth broke into a half smile. As the man dragged himself onto the branch next to Alice, Stanley noted the colourful long waist coat he wore and the long black jacket with full sleeves. At the man's neck was tied a dirty white handkerchief over an even dirtier shirt. The man wore tight woollen breeches tucked into knee high black leather riding boots. Blood dripped slowly down his face which he wiped with the cuff of his long coat. Then he looked at Alice and spoke.

"Now I must've died after all and gone straight to heaven else why am I looking at the face of a lovely angel."

The man's voice was rough and low and Art thought the words sounded like someone from his street, so he said brightly,

"She aint no angel, Mister. She's Alice and she's got lemonade in that bag".

Stan who remembered having the same thought as the man about Alice's angelic ways tried to be sensible and said in a steady voice,

"You're bleeding Mister, what happened and can we help?"

"Grazed at the temple, Sir, by a pistol shot; riding my horse away after I bid farewell to Old Newgate. They gave chase but didn't catch me. I am too quick, too clever to stay as a guest in his Majesty's prison. No leg irons can hold

Gentleman Jack Shepherd as long as he hides his nail in his boot."

And with that Jack drew a long sharp iron nail from a seam in his boot and waved it in the air.

The three boys looked nervous as Jack hid the nail back in the seam of his boot.

Alice opened the canvas bag and poured some lemonade in an old cup. As she looked at the man she said, "Take off your hat and we will wash the wound. I think this lemonade will help but it may sting a bit."

The man did as he was asked, for who could disobey the kind instructions of his angel. Alice took her handkerchief, dipped it, in the pale yellow juice and wiped the wound on the man's neck, cleaning the wound gently. The man took the pretty blue handkerchief and pressed it to his wound. He then took the old cup and drank the rest of the juice.

"Thanks Miss, I'm that thirsty. I rode day and night to get here. I am told there's rich pickings to be had round here. I needs a break from London. Me old mate turned me in to save his neck but I'll get even with him. Blast his eyes. He'll dance on the rope at Tyburn afore me."

Alice poured the man more lemonade and asked calmly, as if this was all a very normal conversation,

"Do you have a plan? Where are you going?"

The man looked at the faces of the children and Stan thought to himself why doesn't he ask who we are and why he should trust us.

Just then, as if reading Stan's thoughts Jack Shepherd opened his long jacket to reveal two pistols tucked neatly in his belt. Freddy had seen similar silver and ivory handled pistols on a school trip to a museum. He had also heard the name Jack Shepherd in his history of London stories.

Then Freddy made his hand into a gun shape, pointed two fingers towards the man and said,

"Stand and Deliver; your money or your life. Are you playing a highwayman in a show, Mister and pinched the props?"

Freddy was laughing now but Stanley, with memories of his encounter with the King, was worried that Freddy might annoy this dangerous man with pistols.

"What year is it Mr Shepherd?"asked Stan quietly.

"Why such a strange question!" the man replied. "It was 1724 when I left London and it still is as far as I know. I need to get to my horse. There's some valuables on her saddle. I need to send her further in the forest so she doesn't give me away. She will come back when I whistle."

Then the man tried to stand to climb down the tree but he slipped back feeling faint through exhaustion and loss of blood. Freddy, who was finding the whole story quite unbelievable, offered to go down the tree, collect the man's valuable bag and bring it to him. That would sort out the truth.

The man looked doubtful but Alice reassured him that all would be well and Freddy could be trusted. Stan would have offered to accompany Freddy but Art was holding tightly to him and looked very scared.

Freddy climbed down the tree suddenly feeling rather important and brave. Sure enough there was the grazing horse. Freddy whispered to the horse using the name Black Bess which sprung to mind from his History stories and stroked her nose. Then he saw a small sack tied to the saddle. He untied the knots and smacked the horse on its flank saying "Fly Bess Fly," just as he had been instructed. The horse trotted deeper into the forest and Freddy pushed the bag into the belt on his shorts as he climbed back into the branches of the tree. Strangely this time the climb was easier and he felt the branches push him gently towards the light of the high tree top.

Freddy felt he had done a brave and helpful thing and he began to feel more like he used to when he played with his little brother, Jack.

Freddy sat back at the top of the tree and passed the bag to the man.

Jack Shepherd reached for the bag, put his hand in and pulled out a gold coin. "Your share, my friend," he said offering the coin to Freddy.

Alice intervened, afraid her cousin would be in trouble with the police if he accepted the coin. She took the coin, noting the head of another King George on the side (not her King George VI) and placed it back in the sack with the others.

"Thanks, Mr Shepherd, but we can't spend that here. You might need it."

Then Alice took a deep breath, looked the man in the eye and asked

"Are you really a highway man?"

The man made a mock bow,

"Honest Jack at your service Ma'am and we prefer to say a Gentleman of the road. I would never rob a pretty lady like yourself; but I may request a dance from you. It's only rich old men who deserve to part up with some wealth. I am well known in London as no jail can hold me. I've escaped 3 times from cell irons and the like. But now I am out of London to keep my neck straight, as you might say. My girl Lizzie Lyons will tell me when to return. She 'll get a message to me somehow."

At this the man rubbed his neck slowly as if to check it was in one piece and looked down.

"There's a phone box in our street, or there was before Hitler and his bombs." said Art, trying to be helpful, "She could phone you, like our Nan phones our mum."

Jack looked puzzled and thought the child was probably a simpleton.

"For now," said Alice, "I think we should have our picnic. Our guest is probably hungry."

And he certainly was. He ate the soft pink meat as he called it and enjoyed the ginger biscuits. He found the food strange but Stan told him it was country fare and he seemed satisfied with that answer.

"Next time you're in London find me at the Black Lion Inn, I'll get you some real victuals. Does the best ale and lamb chops in Drury Lane."

"I've been there, Drury Lane", said Alice, "to the Theatre, with my mother and father for a Christmas treat."

"Yes," agreed Stan, not wanting to be left out, "We're all from London,"

"Then I'm with friends," said Jack and lifted his hat for a moment to show his respect.

Then Jack looked around the group and seemed to think for a moment.

"Now as we are friends perhaps you can tell me about the rich houses round here. I can squeeze through a locked door, jemmy a window quiet as a mouse; after candlesticks and a bit of plate. The rich don't miss a thing or two."

Then Jack fixed his eyes on Art and reached out to touch his legs.

"You're a skinny little runt aint you, just right for pushing through those small windows. What you say, want to be Jack's 'prentice? Better than the poor 'ouse. I done a stint in there as a kid", and the man spat and wiped his mouth on his sleeve.

Art looked terrified and clung harder to Stan. He was careful to keep Rabbit out of sight as he had begun to understand that this man was a robber who wanted treasure, and Rabbit might be in danger of being stolen.

Alice sat up straight and once again smiled sweetly at Jack.

"No thanks," she said "Art has a family and works on a farm at the moment. He can't help you with your business".

Stan was again lost in admiration at the bold Alice and was just about to add his view that his Aunt would be looking for them when Freddy shouted.

"No but I can help you, Mister. The Church has got a gold plate and a big silver cup. I seen it, we have it out at Church on a Sunday".

"Freddie, stop." Said Alice looking horrified, "What would your mummy say if she heard you?"

Freddy blushed and looked down. He was thinking of the thrill of riding on Bess and being a highwayman rather than the horrible act of stealing from a Church.

"Sorry," he muttered, "Just a bit of excitement."

"Just how I started, son," said Jack. "Just a bit of excitement. Left my trade as a carpenter but that helped me with my new trade as a gentleman of the road. I knew about escaping when I was caught. They all came to see me in jail, the rich and the famous. They all wanted to know how I did it, how I escaped".

Jack then told them of his most famous escape from Newgate when Lizzie had brought in clothes to disguise him as a woman and how he had sawed out a bar from the window, squeezed through and lowered them both down to the ground on rags tied together."

The children listened in awe.

Jack then declared he had to go and find his horse before anyone suspected where he was hiding. Again he made a mock bow and removed his tri-cornered hat for a few seconds.

"Thank you, my friends," he said," for your help and the vit'les. Remember, Black Lion Inn, Drury Lane, for our next meeting."

Quickly Freddy said, "I ll help you find your horse Mister; she likes me" and he followed the man down the tree to the ground.

Alice was quick to start her descent from the tree as she was worried that Freddy was too enthralled by the Highwayman's tales of adventure and might be tempted to join him.

Shadows from the afternoon sun were now falling around the tree and casting gloomy shapes on the grass and ferns. Freddy watched as Jack whistled a shrill pitch whistle and as Bess appeared through the trees and nuzzled her master. Jack mounted his horse and re-secured the bag of gold coins to his saddle.

Then he rode off through the trees calling back to Freddy,

"Thanks for the tip, my friend, I am obliged."

Freddy looked after him and as he gazed, he caught sight of a glint in the fading sun. He bent down and picked up the gold coin that had fallen from the bag as Jack rode off. He put the coin in the pocket of his shorts and decided that he could tell the others later.

Soon Alice, Stan and Art had reached the ground. Just then there was a gentle thud and the lost football plopped onto the grass.

"I nearly forgot about the ball," said Freddy, "That's why we climbed the tree. How odd we didn't see it as we climbed."

"Not really", Stan muttered, "because you kicked the ball into the tree in a different century".

"Well, this has been a strange picnic and adventure," mused Alice to Stanley.

Then Stanley told Alice about the meeting with King Charles while Freddy and Art kicked the ball to each other.

"You do believe me don't you?" said Stanley looking at Alice's frown as she listened.

"I do now, Stanley. There must be an explanation for these strange things. My father says everything can be explained by science if we use it properly. He says it will win us the war. Let's try to think logically."

Alice was right about science and winning the war but was wrong to overlook magic and its mysterious forces.

The children were feeling tired and began to walk back to the forest path when they heard Auntie Nell calling them and were soon faced with Gwen jumping up and licking their faces.

Freddy thought about Stan's comment that he had kicked the ball in a different time and so he put his hand in his pocket to see if the gold coin was still there. Much to his surprise the hard round coin pressed into his hand.

Auntie Nell was surprised to see the older children were quiet and thoughtful although Art jumped and skipped towards her. Gwen was excited to see Freddy and tried to grab the ball. Freddy laughed, feeling glad that Gwen had chosen him to play.

The children returned to the cottage where Molly Brown was waiting to take home Alice and Freddy for supper. Then Molly mentioned to Auntie Nell the possibility of seeing them at the Church Service the next day. The older children stared at the ladies as Molly said,

"When is the Vicar going to have our goblet and plate repolished; such an ancient dent in the cup and a nasty dent in the plate. You'd think after a couple of hundred years the Church could afford the repair. Such a silly story that a robber tried to steal them but they fell from his saddle as he rode off. Anyone would think we had a highwayman here in the forest. Just laziness if you ask me".

Freddy went pale as he thought to himself that Jack had tried to steal the Church treasure, after all. Perhaps he should tell the others about the gold coin, still in his pocket. Stan and Alice looked at each other as Alice said,

"There must be an answer, Stan. Let's get our thinking caps on".

"Well," said Auntie Nell softly, "It was a long time ago, so we'll never know for certain, but we know these children aren't the first visitors from London to come here for safety."

Stan whispered to Alice, "I think we do know for certain. Glad Jack didn't succeed this time."

Molly drove her charges home with Alice thinking hard about time and whether the old oak Tree had somehow absorbed and stored its memories as it grew straight and strong over the centuries. Freddy touched the gold coin in his trouser pocket and wondered what he should do with it.

CHAPTER 8: ANOTHER CLIMBING BOY

And so the four children continued to build the daily routine of going to school and meeting up in the play ground. Auntie Nell commented on how bright and educated Rabbit had become now that Art was teaching him how to read. Stan and Alice were allowed to start a project on trees and their teacher encouraged them to draw the complex root map of a tree. Alice told her teacher that she believed trees were able to communicate with each other and she believed they had memories. Miss Taylor smiled and said the idea was a strange one. Years later Alice was proved to be right about the communication skills of trees. Science discovered that trees gave off chemicals to talk to each other about safety and other things.

Freddie was more interested in football than trees but was beginning to feel better about other people. Freddie had continued to look at the gold coin he had found. He didn't tell the others but much to everyone's surprise had asked Molly when the next Sunday service would be held in the old Church as he would like to attend. Molly decided that Freddy was asking to say a prayer for his family and so arranged to take Alice and Freddy to the Service the next Sunday morning. When she told her friend, Nellie, it was decided that Nellie would accompany them with Stan and Art. It was also agreed that they would all have lunch together and that the children could play in the forest for the afternoon.

"It's getting cooler now Molly," said Nellie, "We should let the children play out now before the Autumn brings bad weather."

"Good idea, my friend", replied Molly, "See you in Church on Sunday."

Sunday arrived and the Church Service began at 11am with the children and their Aunties sitting quietly in the front pew. Auntie Nellie always had Mint Imperial sweets with her for such solemn occasions. Each child was given a little white sugary mint sweet to suck as Auntie Nell promised it would help with their prayers. She knew it would also help them not giggle and nudge each other during the Vicar's rather boring sermon.

Freddie had volunteered to take the gold plate around the pews for the small number of people in the congregation to give some money for the Church upkeep. At the end of the collection Freddie took the gold coin from his trouser pocket and slid it under the ten shilling note which a farmer had donated. He then walked in the most serious and dignified manner he could summon towards the Vicar and placed the plate of money by his side.

(Only later in the week did the news buzz around the village that an unknown rich benefactor had donated an antique coin to the Church which would be auctioned so the Church could benefit from repairs.) On hearing this Freddie practiced his most surprised and bewildered expression but secretly jumped up and down with relief and pleasure that he had helped Jack Shepherd, the Highwayman, pay for his attempted robbery.

After lunch that Sunday afternoon, the four children, Rabbit and the beloved football set off into the Forest. Freddie kicked and bounced the ball behind the other three children, knowing it would be easy to catch them up. Alice and Stan were in serious discussion about the likelihood of meeting any more of the Oak tree's memories. Art danced Rabbit along as he skipped ahead. It was the same path as before, leading into the shadowy parts of the forest, bordered by ferns and clumps of small, yellow wild flowers. Art picked some of these and tucked them through holes in Rabbit's waistcoat,

"Now you look a bit smarter, Rabbit," Art whispered.

Just then Stanley became aware of the strange magnetic pull of the Tree and heard the low whispering of the wind through the branches:

Riddle-me, Riddle- Me, Riddle-Me Ree,
Climb up my branches and see what I see,
Riddle-me ,Riddle –me Riddle-me Row,
Climb up my branches and know what I know.

Stan turned to Alice, "Can you hear that whispering, Alice?" he asked.

Alice nodded. "We are being called, Stan," she said, "I've thought hard about it and our Tree calls when someone needs help. We're on duty Stan, just like our parents". And she gave Stan a mock salute. Stan smiled and felt even more admiration for his friend.

Art was skipping ahead of his brother and Alice. He saw the old oak Tree set back off the path and also felt the magnetic pull towards its branches. He skipped towards the Tree and leaned against the huge trunk under the dark shadows of the canopy. As he walked around the trunk to the darker side of the tree he heard some gentle sobbing. There sat a little girl with a tattered shawl tied around her shoulders. She had buried her face into the shawl as she wept. Art noted she wore a patched skirt and had bare, dirty feet. Art remembered how awful it was to feel sad and afraid so he decided to sit next to her to see if he could help like his big brother helped him.

"Hello little girl," he said, "I'm Art and this is my best friend Rabbit."

The little girl lifted her face and Art could see where her tears had made tracks through the dirt on her cheeks.

"Do you want to hold Rabbit?" Art asked the child. "He always makes me feel better."

The girl pushed her long, tangled dirty blond hair away from her face and reached out a mucky hand for Rabbit. Art gasped when he saw how filthy the child was and started to regret letting her hold Rabbit. However the girl took Rabbit and nursed him under her chin as she held him close. Slowly the little girl stopped sobbing and rubbed her tears on Rabbit's ears. Art managed to say nothing although he knew Rabbit would need a wash when he got home. He noticed the child had very bright blue eyes, the only part of her which didn't seem grey with grime.

"What's wrong, little girl?" asked Art, trying to sound like his big brother. "Are you lost?"

The child looked at him,

"I can't find my brother, Kit. We ran from the Sweep master. He's going to kill Kit, I knows he will; he is so small. Kit hid just here and now I can't find him."

The girl began to cry again and Art started to worry about Rabbit's ears which were becoming very wet and droopy.

"Alice and Stan will know what to do." Said Art, feeling increasingly concerned about Rabbit, "they are very brainy and will help you."

As he spoke, Stan and Alice appeared around the tree and stared at the two children sitting in the shadows of the branches. Alice bent down and took the little girl by the hand, helping her to stand. She then took yet another of her pretty blue handkerchiefs from her coat pocket and wiped the child's eyes. Art jumped up, feeling rather important that he was the first to know just what had happened to the little girl. He told the other two,

"She's lost her little brother, Kit. I lent her Rabbit to make her better. A bad man with a sweeping brush is going to kill them."

The girl looked up at Alice and whispered, " Master Sweep, Hardstone; he owns us. We was placed by the Beadle from the orphanage with him and his missus. Kit 's 'prenticed to him, to learn to climb chimneys and clean them. But he can't do it; he's too weak to climb. The Master beats him to make him climb."

Alice went pale as she stared at the child's dirty, tear-stained face and Stan started to feel a bit sick.

"We'll help you find brother." said Stan, "What's your name?"

"My Ma used to call me Joany but the Missus calls me Thing."

"Joany", said Alice, "That's a lovely name. We will help you, Joany."

Joany looked at Alice and her eyes filled with tears again. It was a long time since she had heard her name used in such a kind way.

At that moment the tree began to sway and murmur. Stan touched the trunk.

"It wants us to climb," said Stan. "It wants to help."

Stan helped Joany onto the lower branches of the Oak. Then, to his surprise the little girl seemed to swiftly climb to the wide comfortable branches at the tree top. Art followed, having retrieved a rather soggy and grubby Rabbit from Joany. Soon the four children were safely in the arms of the old Tree. Then Alice remembered Freddy and was worried he would not find them.

"He will," said Stan, "the Tree will call him."

Freddy had taken his time to follow the others along the path. He was pleased with his football skills and practiced kicking and heading the ball as he walked along, ducking in and out of the trees as he moved forward. He chased his ball into the bushes as he headed it too far. Then he stopped quickly. In front of him, holding the ball in his outstretched arms was a small, very dirty looking child. The little boy had a black stained face and soot stained clothes. He wore a tight cap which had a faded sweep's badge on the band. His knee length breeches were also black with soot as were his skinny legs and rough leather shoes. Freddy noted that the boy's knees were scabbed with old cuts and dried fresh blood stained his shins. He could also see the same bloody scabs on his elbows. Freddy stared at the boy and could not believe the sorry state the child was in. For a moment Freddy remembered the body of his little brother after the bombing raid had killed him. His face and clothes were also dirty and blackened but not like this child.

The boy handed the ball to Freddy and was going to run off but Freddy touched his arm and said , "Would you like to have a little play of the ball?"

The boy seemed unsure but when Freddy kicked the ball to him, he kicked it back with a small unsteady movement.

"What are you doing here? Are you lost?" Freddy inquired gently.

The boy shook his head and whispered, "Hiding from Master; he's going to stick me some more." Then the child lifted his shirt and showed Freddy some deep red welts still painful from the beating he had taken.

Freddy felt upset and angry at this and was determined to protect this boy, as he remembered he had not been able to protect his little brother.

"That's not right," he said, "What's your name? Where are your mum and dad?"

"I'm Kit; aint got no ma or a pa. I belong to the Master."

Then Kit explained to Freddy that he and his sister, Joany, were placed in the orphanage workhouse after their mother died. When he was 6 years old he had been taken to a court house where he was signed up to be an apprentice chimney sweep to Master Hardstone who had several climbing boys cleaning chimneys in the towns and villages around the area. He explained to Freddy how he was asked to wedge himself in the chimney at an angle and push himself up using his elbows and knees which became scraped and bled. The brush was attached to the top of his cap to loosen the soot which fell below into the hearth of the big houses.

"I got scared, Mister," Kit said anxiously. "Another climbing boy, Joe, got stuck; they lit a fire under him to make him shift but he was jammed. Master tried to push me up to pull on Joe's legs but I couldn't do it. Master got mad and beat me with a stick. Joe was dead when they pulled him out."

Then Kit told Freddie his sister had seen what had happened. It was her job to sweep the soot and help bag it. During the fuss and noise over Joe and the Constable being sent for they ran away and had come to the Forest to hide. He was looking for Joany as they had become separated.

Freddie could not believe what he was hearing. He had heard about climbing boys in his history lessons at school and gradually he realised that this child was from another time. But Freddy knew he had to help, if only he knew how.

At that moment the wind through the branches became stronger, the whispering trees called to them and Freddy felt the pull towards the old Oak tree. He took Kit by the hand and let him carry the ball in his other arm.

"Come on, Kit," he said, feeling like the strong big brother he was meant to be, "come and meet my friends. We'll find a way to help you and your sister."

Freddy heard the whispering getting more forceful as the magnetic pull of the tree guided him and Kit to its branches.

Freddy helped Kit climb onto the branches of the Tree and followed up behind him as the whispering became calmer and Freddy knew he had done the right thing. This time he was aware of the branches pushing him forward. He could hear Alice and the others talking and he called up to them that he was coming and that Kit was with him.

The two orphans hugged each other while Freddy and Alice swapped the stories they had been given. Stanley felt very concerned and worried that these visitors from the past were becoming harder to help.

Art was also worried, especially that he might have to share Rabbit with Kit as well as Joany.

CHAPTER 9: KIT AND JOANY

And so the Tree held six children safely in its large, gentle branches.

Kit and Joany held hands and shivered. Freddy asked Alice if there was any food in the canvas bag which the children could eat. Alice opened the bag and found a tin of little lemon cakes which Auntie Nell had packed for their picnic. She offered a cake to the brother and sister and watched as their grimy little hands took the food and how they slowly began to lick and suck at the sweetness of the cakes.

Then both children began to cry again .

"We aint had nothing like this Miss," said Joany. "So lovely."

Stanley looked at Art and thought that he and Kit were similar ages but Art was bigger and stronger. Stan was beginning to feel lost for ideas. He wondered to himself how it was possible to help two poor, neglected orphans from a different day and time.

Alice was thinking something similar and wondered about the year the children were living in. She looked at Joany and asked,

"Joany, I wonder if you know the name of our King or Queen just now?"

" I knows", said Kit, "I seen her picture on the wall of the house where we sweep. Master says she's awatching of me and will come for me for the Tower if I don't work at the flues."

"Queen Victoria," said Freddy excitedly, "They're Victorians."

"That's right Sir," said Joany, "Queen Victoria, she's our Queen."

Alice looked thoughtful and said to Stanley, "I think there were Acts of Parliament to stop them using children for labour. Just not sure how we can help. It's so cruel!"

"We've got to do something," whispered Freddy to Alice. "Kit won't survive. Look at the scrapes on his legs and arms. Look how thin and dirty they both are." Once again Freddy thought of his little brother Jack and began to feel desperate.

Art had been watching the others and was careful to keep Rabbit out of sight in case anyone suggested that he gave his friend to Kit to make him feel better. He was surprised by the gloomy, puzzled faces of the older children and their lack of ideas, so he decided he would have the first good idea.

"I think we need a growed-up," said Art in quite a loud voice which surprised everyone, including Art himself. "Auntie

Nellie will know how to wash off the black stuff in that nice tin bath she has. She knows how to do everything."

(Art particularly enjoyed bath night in the old tin bath in front of Nell's log fire. Next to his Mum and Dad, Auntie Nell was his favourite grown-up).

"Great idea, Art," said Stan. Then he turned to Alice and Freddy to discuss his concerns that the memory of the tree would not stretch back to Nellie's cottage.

"As we walk along the path towards our cottage I think the children will fade and disappear.

Don't we have to be here near the Tree and its memories to stay in their time?"

"Well," said Freddy, "Kit was quite a way from here when I found him. Let's try and see what happens."

Alice explained to Kit and Joany that they must climb down the tree and that they would find a nice lady who would help them. The orphans looked fearful.

"He'll get me," cried Kit, "Master will get me and stick me."

"He won't," said Freddy fiercely, "I won't let him. Here, hold our ball. It always makes things right."

Despite the seriousness of the situation, Art was beaming with pleasure and confidently led the way down the tree.

"At last," he was thinking to himself, "My idea was a good one and the others thought it was good and worth doing."

Art landed first on the ground and leaned against the huge trunk whilst whispering to Rabbit,

"We're important, Rabbit, we're having ideas, good ideas. They're listening to us."

Freddy and Stan helped the orphans to the ground and Alice was soon beside them.

Then Alice took the blue ribbon from her hair and tied it onto Joany's wrist. She asked Stan to tie the other end to her own wrist.

"I think the ball and the ribbon might help the children stay with us," said Alice. "I wonder if objects are a sort of link between the ages." Alice was looking for a scientific theory that would help them know how to do the right thing.

"Like the pyramids telling us about ancient Egypt," added Stanley, hoping that Alice would be impressed at his thinking.

Alice looked at the others and said, "I think we must all hold hands as we go along the path to keep together in Time".

Stanley was pleased to take Alice's hand in his left hand and Kit's hand in his right hand. Freddy held Kit's other hand and tucked the football under Kit's arm. Joany held tightly to Alice's hand and the blue ribbon tying them together. Art held Joany's free hand and Rabbit's paw in his other hand. In this way the children formed a strong wall of determination, ready to solve any problems they might meet.

The children started their journey along the forest path towards Auntie Nell's cottage. Stanley thought the path appeared to change as they walked, becoming thick with plants and bushes. Just then they saw the cottage in the distance with a curl of smoke rising into the sky which was darkening for the late afternoon. As they approached the gate Art shouted,

"We're lost, this aint our cottage. Where's our house?"

Stan and Alice stared at the cottage. It was the same little thatched house with low windows and doors but it was also very different. There was no wall separating it from the road which was now small and narrow. Vegetables were growing alongside the house under the windows. There was a wooden fenced enclosure on the other side where Auntie's old car had been parked. From behind the fence they could hear the grunts of a pig.

"Where's the car?" asked Stan, feeling very nervous. "And when did we get a pig!!"

The children walked into the garden, just as the low front door opened and a woman stepped out with tin bucket in her hand. Surely it was Auntie Nellie. Stan noticed the same kind face but gone were her greying short curls. This woman had her hair tied up in a bun on top of her head. She had a long sleeved blouse covered with a shawl tied at the waist. Even stranger was the long green skirt she wore and coarse cotton pinafore.

Stan summoned courage and let go, rather reluctantly, of Alice's hand. He called to the woman who was walking towards the pig stye (for that was what the wooden enclosure was),

"Auntie Nell, We're back, we're home".

The woman turned and stared at them,

"Who's wearing my name out? Well goodness me what a funny little bunch of ragamuffins you are. Are you lost? People often get lost in the forest and come here to ask the way."

The woman spoke with a country accent, like Auntie Nell's but much stronger.

Then Art began to cry into Rabbit's ears as he thought they had lost another home. He whispered to Stan,

"This is our house, we live here with Auntie Nellie. Where is she? Where's her car?"

"I am Nellie, lived here all my life since I was born. My daughter's Nellie too but she's away working as a dairy maid in Manor Farm. You don't live here, my ducks, but come in and we will see where your folks are."

Stan remembered what their Auntie Nell had told him about the cottage and how it had been in the family for generations. This must be the Grandmother of Nellie Winter. They had managed it. They had managed to leave the circle of the Tree and stay in the time of the orphans. But how, he thought to himself, could they explain this to the kind woman smiling at them.

Granny Nellie (for grandmother to Nellie Winter she was) invited the children to enter the cottage and sit in the kitchen around the old range where a warm fire was flickering. Kit and Joany sat on the floor and warmed their hands at the grate. Alice, Freddy and Stan sat on an upright wooden settle with Art squashed on the end.

Then Granny Nellie looked at Kit and the bleeding scabs on his arms and legs. She also looked at his sooty appearance and the dirty hair and face of Joany. She noticed the other boys and the older girl were clean and nicely, if a little oddly, dressed.

"Well you're a funny bunch of chicks, I must say. Where'd you get hurt like that ?" she asked Kit bending down to look at his scabs.

Alice decided it was time to speak and try to take charge. She looked into Granny Nellie's thoughtful gaze and spoke clearly and with the confidence her mother had taught her.

"Dear Miss Nellie, I am sorry we have surprised you. We thought we had an Aunt living here and we came to ask for help. I am Alice. Me, Freddy, Stanley and Art are not from around here." Alice gestured toward the others on the bench who each smiled weakly at the woman as their name was mentioned.

Alice went on to explain that they had been travelling in the forest when they met Kit and Joany. Alice knew she had Granny Nellie's complete attention when she sat down in the wooden rocking chair at the kitchen table and wiped her face with her shawl.

Alice told the story of the orphans, the terrible tale of Joe who had died in the chimney whilst being forced to sweep it.

"They've run away from the Master sweep. We want to help but don't know how. Do you know what we should do?"

Granny Nellie wiped her eyes on the corner of her shawl. She had heard similar stories in the village and town, especially about the little boy Joe whose funeral was to be a pauper's one in the local church as he belonged to that Parish.

Granny focussed her attention on the little children by the fire. Stan was again lost in admiration for the clever Alice but thought it odd that the other Nellie did not ask about them.

"First things first," said Granny Nellie. Then she poured the hot water from the kettle on the range into a bowl and placed it on the large wooden table. Then she got some soft cotton cloths and began to bathe Kit's scrapes. Finally she washed the faces of both children.

"There now," she said softly, "The Good Lord can see what little angels he has here."

The peaceful moment did not last. There came a hammering on the door and a man's voice shouting,

"Open up Mrs Nell. There's reports of scum, nasty pauper kids hiding your way. You could be in danger."

At that moment the door opened suddenly and a skinny short man, wearing a great coat that was far too big for him, fell through onto the floor. His large hat flew off his head and landed in the blackened water which Granny Nellie had placed by the door ready to be thrown away.

Even though the situation was dire, Alice, Freddy and Stan couldn't help but giggle at the sight. But Kit and Joany went pale and ran to Alice and Freddy for protection. They had recognised the Beadle who had sold them to Master Hardstone.

CHAPTER 10: BEADLE BEGONE

The Beadle stood up, grabbed his hat from the dirty water and wiped it with his sleeve before placing the hat on his head. He drew himself up to his full height and tried to look important. But then the dirty water from the wet hat began to drip black trails down his face, spoiling the image he was trying to create. The children giggled again as he removed his hat and placed it on the wooden table.

The Beadle's great coat and cocked hat had belonged to the previous Beadle who was a much bigger man. They had been passed to him when he had been appointed by the Parish to manage their affairs, especially the control of the poor.

Granny Nellie knew the man well. As she passed him a cloth to dry his face she said,

"Well Mr Birt, a fine Beadle you are; two lost children and one dead one stuck up a chimney so I hear. What have you been a-doing of? You are supposed to visit them and check aren't you? Doesn't the law say that orphans have to be washed once a week and brought to Sunday school every week for to know their Bible. I haven't seen these two in church on one occasion".

Mr Birt, ran his fingers around his tight collar and stared at the two small children trying to hide behind the others on the bench. He knew he must get hold of them and return them to Mr Hardstone and his wife, but he was beginning to feel nervous and fearful for his position in the Parish. There was talk around the Council of all children by law having to go to school and the licensing of sweeps.

"I have tried, Mrs Nell," said the Beadle smiling weakly. "I have visited but the 'prentices are out early in the morning, calling 'Soot-oh, Sweep'. You must have heard them. Too early for me; I haven't managed to see them. Anyway they don't like getting washed and what would the Vicar say if dirty orphans turned up for Sunday school amongst decent folk. Now I will just take them from you and leave you in peace."

The children held their breath and Kit and Joany clung tighter to Alice and Freddy.

Granny Nell folded her arms, stuck out her chin and said,

"You will do no such thing, Mr Birt. Look at that state of them; look at the cuts and bruises on that little mite. What are we, heathens? What is the Good Lord thinking looking down on us", Granny Nell was raising her voice now and getting quite red in the face.

"Remember your Bible, Mr Birt. Suffer the little children to come unto me, dirty faces or not!"

Mr Birt looked down and said the Parish had paid good money to the Hardstones to raise the children and teach them a trade. Granny Nell lowered her voice and told the Beadle that the feeling in the village was that he wasn't keeping to the law and that the burial of little Joe in a pauper's grave was likely to cause trouble. If he knew what was good for him he would seek release of the children from the Magistrate and find them new homes.

The Beadle knew that Mrs Nell was right. The Constable had said Mr Hardstone needed to answer to the Magistrate to prove Joe's death was an accident. He would not be allowed to use any more sweeping boys until the Court had cleared him.

"1870 and we're using little children like slaves. May the Lord have mercy on us!" said Granny Nell. " I will keep the children here until you get it done. Little Joany can learn to be a dairy maid with my daughter. They want more hands on the farm. When Kit is stronger he can be placed as a groom or something else. Take your hat and go."

The Beadle picked up his hat, careful not to place it on his head this time, but he did not see the bucket of pig swill left by the cottage door and tripped over it. He left with the sticky mixture all over his shoes and leggings.

The children stood up and clapped Granny Nell, laughing at Mr Birt as he slid along the old road towards the Church.

" Hooray, Mrs Nell, hooray," Freddy shouted, jumping up and down, "You have saved Kit and Joany. Thank you".

"You saved them first, what brave children you are." said Granny Nell quietly. " Now it is getting dark, you had better be getting to your homes. Your folk will be missing you. Don't worry about these little souls. I promise you I will take care of them and make sure they have a better life. May God forgive us." Granny Nell put an arm around each child and Kit and Joany smiled and snuggled into her warm apron.

Alice said goodbye to Joany and put the blue hair ribbon into her hand.

"It will bring you luck, Joany," she said.

Much to Alice's surprise, Freddy offered the football to Kit but he shook his head and said

"Thank you Freddy for saving my life."

Freddy felt a huge wave of relief as his guilt over his little brother faded.

Art felt Rabbit was better off with him and so tucked him deep into his pocket.

"Come on everyone", called Stan, "We must hurry back along the path towards our Tree, before it gets dark."

Granny Nell, Kit and Joany went back into the warmth of the cottage and closed the door as Stan, Alice, Freddy and Art began to run along the path back towards the Forest.

This time Stan could not hear the wind whispering to him or feel the magnetic pull of the Tree.

The path then began to look more familiar.

"Do you think we are back in 1940?" Stan said to the others as they stopped for breath.

"We did it Stan," said Alice, "We stayed with the children in their time. I think we met Auntie Nellie's grandmother. What a wonderful woman!"

Freddy looked troubled. "Do you think she will really be able to help Kit and Joany? That Beadle seemed to think she would have to hand them over."

"Yes I do," said Stanley, again remembering his history, "Times were changing then. Poor children were getting more help."

Art did not want to be left out and reminded the others about his good idea to find Auntie Nell.

"You were the cleverest and bravest of us all, Art," said Stan "You and Rabbit deserve a medal!"

"Yes", said Art, " but I'd rather have our little cottage back and our Auntie Nell. I 'm scared it's gone away, like Dad and our London home".

Just as Stanley began to realise that Art was really settling in to their new home, he heard voices calling to them. It was Auntie Nellie and Molly coming towards them along the Forest path. And then Gwen rushed into view, grabbed Rabbit, from Art's pocket and everyone started to laugh.

"We were getting worried about you," said Auntie Nell, "We couldn't find you earlier. I think you all must have had quite an adventure."

The children looked at each other and agreed they had.

CHAPTER 11: NOW
WE ARE SEVEN

Auntie Nellie noticed how quiet and tired Stanley and Art were for the next few days. They asked her some strange questions. Art wanted to know if she had ever kept a pig. Auntie Nellie thought for a moment and then remembered about Big Cecil, the large pink porker her Grandmother had kept for years. Nellie laughed as she told the children that she had never met Cecil but heard all about him from her Mother. Especially how her Granny had become so fond of Cecil the pig that he was never turned into bacon and pork chops but remained with the family until he was very old.

"My Grandmother and Mother kept son of Cecil when I was small. What a noise he used to make, grunting and snorting. I was very little then and I was quite scared of him." mused Auntie Nell.

"Is that why your Granny built the big shed around him to keep you safe? And what was in the big tin bucket full of slops?" asked Art, still remembering his awful fear during the rescue of Kit and Joany, that the beloved little cottage that had become his home had gone.

"Well, bless you Art,"said Nellie looking surprised, "I had forgotten the old bucket Granny used to feed Cecil and son of Cecil. How did you know about our pigs? My car stands there now where the old shed used to be and it's as much trouble as Mister Cecil was and as noisy!"

Art looked worried as he remembered that Stanley had told him to say nothing about their strange adventure. Stanley butted in.

"Auntie Nell, didn't you tell us about your Granny; I am not sure if you mentioned Cecil. I don't suppose you have a photograph of her at all and the cottage as it was."

"What a nice idea, Stanley," and with that Nellie reached to the back of some books piled on the nearby shelf and retrieved an ancient looking sepia photograph. There, outside the low cottage door, stood the kind lady the children had turned to for help with Joany and Kit. Stanley held the photograph and studied the long dress, heavy apron and straggling grey hair, tied in a bun.

"She's old there; it was taken just before I was born, and I only knew her for a short time." explained Auntie Nell. "I was called after her, as was my Mother. Granny was known for her kindness my mother told me. She often helped travellers who had got lost. There is a story, but I don't know if it's true, that she helped two little orphans who were in a sorry state. Also that she went to the Magistrate's Court to give evidence in some sort of Parish business. I don't know any more. My mother said it was all a strange affair and I don't know the names of the orphans or what happened to them."

Art was about to say that he knew the names were Joany and Kit when Stan interrupted him and gave him a fierce glare.

"What an interesting story, Auntie and your Grandmother sounds like a wonderful person. We might find some answers about the orphans at school or in the Church grave yard."

Art looked down and muttered that he and Rabbit knew the names and that Granny was wonderful.

Auntie Nell asked the boys to sit down with her at the kitchen table where she poured them some milk. She took a letter from her pocket and held it up.

"I have a surprise for you both. Your mother has written and she is coming to visit for the day. Art did you remember you are going to be 7 years old next Saturday. We're going to have a little party for you and best of all, your mummy is coming. She's driving your Uncle's car all the way from Kent where she's working on his farm. Are you excited?"

Art looked confused. He didn't like the idea of being 7 years old. He had decided to stay at six and to try to keep everything the same until his Dad got home. He didn't say anything but screwed up his face and pushed Rabbit under his chin. He wondered if Stanley and he would go home with his Mum, just as he was getting used to his new little house.

Stanley watched his brother and guessed what he was thinking.

"Art, it will be fun. Mum has gone to work on Uncle Walter's farm as a Land Girl. It's great that she's out of London, away from the bombs. We will stay here with Auntie Nell and Alice and Freddy until it's safe to go home to London. We can show her our school and our Forest. It will be so good to see her."

For all his big brother ways, Stanley started to feel tearful and homesick. He longed for a hug from his Mother and to be her best big boy again. Auntie Nellie was surprised at the boys' reactions but declared that their mother was bringing Art's favourite chocolate cake and that she would try to find a candle so he could make a birthday wish.

"Oh and Auntie Molly is coming with your two friends. What a party we will have, next Saturday."

Art whispered to Rabbit that they were going to be seven and that it would be alright, especially with a chocolate birthday cake to look forward to.

Art looked at Stanley and said, "Will she remember us Stanley? What if mum's forgotten who we are".

"No fear of that Art," said Nellie softly, "She's knitting Rabbit a new yellow waistcoat. In her letter she tells me that she thinks about the three of you, everyday and longs to give you hugs and kisses."

Art and Stanley thanked Auntie Nell and began to look forward to the next Saturday when their Mother would arrive.

It seemed ages to Art before his birthday arrived, although it was just a few days which he spent trying to be very good in school, in case the frightening Miss Simpkins got to meet his mother. Art studied himself several times in the old cracked bedroom mirror. He wanted to see the signs in his appearance that would mean he was changing from 6 to 7 years old. No matter how hard he stared at himself there was the same pale face, brown eyes and sandy mop of hair he had known for a long time.

"Well Rabbit," Art confided to his friend, " I can't see any sign of being 7. I think it's not going to be very different from being 6. Just as well, 'cause Mum might not know it's us if we change too much and Dad might wonder who we are......when he comes home."

Just to check on this, Art found his big brother in Auntie's sitting room where she had allowed him to look through all the old and some new books on her shelves. Despite thinking that he didn't need any more school, Stan was finding lots of interesting things to read. He enjoyed the history books and encyclopaedias he found and strangely he wanted to know more and more. Auntie Nellie had remarked that he was becoming a proper scholar and that his mum would be so proud that he was becoming so clever. Stan had felt a little embarrassed as he didn't want to be a 'swot' and get teased like some of the boys in his London school and anyway he wanted to be a motor bike mechanic like his Dad.

" Strange," he thought to himself, "but these books call me just like that old Tree."

At that moment, it all seemed odd to Stanley, but when he grew up he knew he had received a great gift as a child and he continued to teach others that there was no knowing the future without understanding the past.

Art found Stan with his nose in a book about Vikings. He went close to his brother and tried to look at the pictures in the book. They weren't so scary, he thought, if you looked at them upside down.

"Stan," Art said to his brother, " Do I look 7 yet? Rabbit and me have looked in the mirror everyday this week but we're just the same. No sign of 7 coming."

Stan laughed, "You've definitely grown Artie," he said, "look where your shorts are now, above your knees. They used to be below your knees. Anyone can see you are 7. And anyway we've had adventures and that makes us very special, smart boys."

Art beamed his best smile. He felt taller and braver and without a doubt like a 7 year old boy.

Saturday and the birthday was here at last. Stan and Art had clean jumpers and shirts and both tried to stick down their unruly hair with water. Auntie Nellie had laid the big table with a large white cloth which had flowers embroidered on it by her mother. She put out pretty plates, sandwiches and little cakes. In the middle was a china cake stand awaiting the chocolate birthday cake.

Such excitement when Mum arrived. She climbed out of the old Morris Sedan car and ran to hug and kiss her boys. Stan thought how lovely mum looked. She had a new coat and hat and her hair curled up in rolls on her head.

Auntie Nellie stood back at first, smiling her greeting as she leaned on the half opened door. For once Gwen obeyed the order to wait before bounding forward to join in the hugging and kissing. Then there were tears and laughter and everyone talking at once.

"Oh my best boys," said Mum, holding Stan and Art at arm's length, "How you've grown and pink cheeks as well. This place is doing you a world of good. Thank you Miss Winter. How well you have taken care of these two."

Nellie smiled and asked to be called by her first name. She spoke of the pleasure to have the boys' company and how interesting and well-behaved they were.

Then Mum produced an amazing chocolate cake with a big number 7 made of little iced flowers in the middle. It was placed in the centre of the table on the china cake stand and everyone clapped and said how wonderful it was. When Molly, Alice and Freddy arrived, they all sat down for tea. Molly had brought a red candle in a holder for Art to blow out and make a wish.

"You wouldn't know there was a war on," said Molly laughing.

And there were presents to unwrap. Art found he had some new clothes from his mum, some sweets and a book about pirates. Freddy and Alice gave him a colouring book and some fine sharp colouring pencils. Then Molly said she had a special present and produced a toy motor bike from her bag. This had been carved in wood and had once been painted in black and silver. Attached to it was a little wooden sidecar which could be hooked on to the side of the motorbike. Auntie Nellie gasped when she saw the model and then pretended to cough to cover her shock.

"It's not new, Artie," Mollie told him. "It belonged to my friend, a long time ago; I believe he made it because he loved his Sunbeam motor cycle so much. But I knew you were an expert on motorbikes with a side car and so would know how to take care of it."

Auntie Molly looked rather sad as she remembered how her beloved Captain Frank Winter had ridden his motorbike often over to her house to visit. They had been sweethearts before the First World War had started. Auntie Nell was quiet as she thought about her brother cutting and carving the model motorbike as a promise to his fiancé, Molly, that he would always come back and find her, despite being sent to France to fight with his regiment.

Art was speechless with delight as he played with the model motorbike. Then he remembered to thank Auntie Molly before trying to sit Rabbit on the saddle and push his paws onto the handlebars. He decided that being 7 years old was turning out all right. Then everyone sang Happy Birthday to Art who insisted they sang again to Rabbit. When it was time to blow out the red candle Art shut his eyes, held up the toy motor bike and wished hard that he would soon ride with Dad again.

Just then Mum handed a parcel to Rabbit. Art undid it for him and there was the bright yellow waistcoat with a button, she had knitted. Art pulled it on over Rabbit' s head and droopy ears. Rabbit was instantly transformed into a very smart animal; one that any 7 year old boy would be proud to have as his friend.

And so the day continued with Alice and Freddy introduced to Mum and lots of talking and questions and laughter. Mum was shown the garden, the chickens,the path to the forest and the road down to the old church.

When it was time for Molly to take home her two charges, Alice whispered to Stan to come into the garden. There she took out a sketch pad from her pocket and showed Stan a sketch she had made of a tiny overgrown grave behind the church.

"Look, Stan, I found it when we were allowed to go out from class to draw yesterday afternoon. Look at the headstone. It's Joe's grave."

Alice was right again. Stan read the writing she had copied.

HERE LIES JOSEPH A CHILD OF THIS PARISH AGED 8 YEARS

SUFFER THE LITTLE CHILDREN TO COME UNTO ME

(Matthew 19. V 14)

0CTOBER 1870

"It did happen Stan; this was the Joe that Kit worked with." Alice whispered. " I am sure Granny Nellie must have chosen that headstone , they were her words. How strange this all is. I wonder if we will ever understand it."

Stan nodded and told Alice they would talk about it again at school. He knew it had all really happened but how it had happened was a different matter.

The boys had had a wonderful day. They were sad to see Mum get in the car to drive away but she told them she would visit again soon.

"It's not safe to be in London now, boys; we're so lucky to have these new homes. I am happy with Uncle Walter and Auntie May; I am trying to see if we can all be there in the farmhouse. Dad is ok and writing to me but we're not allowed to know exactly where he is stationed."

Stan felt guilty when he realised he was quite happy to stay in this interesting new place where past and present got muddled up. Even Art managed to wave goodbye to his mother without too many tears.

Now he was 7 Art knew he must be sensible and nice so he went to Auntie Nellie and kissed her hand as he held it.

"Thank you Auntie, for the best day of my life," he said, "And Rabbit says thank you too."

This time it was Nellie's turn to wipe away some tears.

CHAPTER 12: THE LOVE LETTER

October progressed into Autumn. The days were slightly cooler and gold and brown colours were appearing in the canopy of the Forest. Art had wasted no time in telling Miss Simpkins and the children in his class that he and Rabbit were now 7 years of age and perhaps could move into Stanley's class. Miss Simpkins, who was now a little kinder in her feelings towards the dreaded London children, allowed Art to tell the class about his Mother's visit and best of all to allow Rabbit to show off his new yellow waist coat. This was followed hurriedly by a return to his sleeping bag in case other small children got the idea that bringing a soft toy to school was a good one.

Alice and Stanley continued to impress their teacher, Miss Taylor, with the seriousness of their studies. Miss Taylor agreed that they could conduct research in the Church graveyard and try to trace records about the children whose names they had found. This had given Alice the chance to copy the headstone of Joseph's grave which she had quietly showed to Stan at the end of Art's birthday party.

Stanley, who a short while ago believed he had grown out of school, was reading more history books and how archaeologists dated objects from the past. He was thinking hard about how ancient objects might hold secrets helpful in the present day. " Just like the Tree", he thought to himself.

Freddie's angry attitude towards everyone was diminishing and Miss Taylor noticed that he had become kinder and helpful to some of the smaller children in school. However Freddy's love of football had not changed. He spent much time in the playground demonstrating his abilities to kick, dribble and head his beloved football. Miss Taylor had managed to set up some small goal nets, borrowed from a relative's defunct Scout group so that all the children could have a football game in the playground.

"Sometimes, new blood in an old village can be a good thing," she had said to her colleague, who was not convinced of this.

Stanley and Alice discussed whether they should make another visit to their Tree and its memories before winter set in and made the climb to the top branches much harder. Freddy wasn't sure that he would accompany them. He was still worrying about what had happened to Kit and Joany.

It was the first weekend of the October half term holiday and Alice came to spend the Saturday with Auntie Nellie, Stanley and Art. Molly had arranged to take Freddy to play football with a boys' team in the nearby town and to shop there whilst he played. Freddy was excited and pleased to have this chance to show off his skills.

Stan and Alice asked Auntie Nell if they could walk in the Forest after lunch and she agreed.

"You will need your coats and scarves as it's getting cold. Soon be November." She reminded them. "What about you Art? Are you going or staying here with me?"

Art thought about the question. He was inclined to stay and play in the warm with Rabbit and the beautiful model motor bike but he was a little worried that Alice was becoming very important to his brother, perhaps even more important than him and Rabbit. So he decided he had better go out to play in the Forest with the other two, just to be sure that he was still Stanley's best friend. So Art jumped up, grabbed Rabbit and his motorbike toy and found his coat.

"I'm ready," he shouted, "Let's go".

The three children walked along the Forest path which was now coated in the crunch of the fallen leaves from the nearby trees. The wild flowers were beginning to fade and the ferns to turn golden brown. Nevertheless, the autumn sun made the walk a pleasant one. The trees still formed a dense overhead canopy as the children drew near to the old Oak tree. Stanley felt the magnetic pull of the Tree and the gentle whispering of the wind through its branches but now more faintly than before.

"It's fading, Alice," he said, "Perhaps we have done our duty and the Tree has finished with us."

"Maybe," replied Alice, "but I think there is another story it wants to tell us. Just listen to the wind stirring through the branches. It's getting stronger. What is it saying?"

The wind did seem to be getting stronger and wilder, as the children approached the Tree. Then to their surprise they saw a tall figure of a man, leaning against the tree and trying in the wind to light with matches a small brown cigar. Alice thought how handsome he looked in his army uniform. The man wore a brown jacket with a large dark brown leather belt buckled at the waist. The jacket had deep pockets and gold buttons with regimental insignia carved on them. A brown leather strap crossed diagonally from his shoulder across his chest to a pistol case which was fastened to his belt. He wore leather riding britches which met his large laced up, black boots at his knee. On his head he wore a peaked military cap with a badge at the front. They could see that the top of his shirt was a grey colour and that he had a tie tucked in his jacket. Stanley and Alice realised that this man was an Officer in the Army but what was he doing leaning against their Tree?

Art was running behind Alice waving his toy motor cycle in the air and making engine noises as he imitated his father's motor bike. The Officer stepped forward from the shadows of the tree and put his cigar stub in his pocket.

"Hey, what have you got there?" he called to Art who was rushing by him. "That looks familiar. I think I had a model just like that. My beloved Sunbeam, what a motor bike, she could really shift."

Art stopped and quickly hid the motorbike toy under his coat for safety.

"It's mine," he said, " My Auntie gave it to me for my birthday. I am Art and I am 7 you know and so is Rabbit." Then Art pulled Rabbit from his pocket in the hope that he would distract this man from from his interest in the motorbike.

"Well and a fine Rabbit he is too," said the Officer in kindly tones. Stan noted that the Man's accent was similar to that of Auntie Nell's. "Could I just look at the little bike for a minute? I used to have one at home. I will give it back."

Art felt very uncertain but took the wooden model from his coat and handed it to the man. The Officer looked at it carefully and smiled. "Just like the one I made a while ago but this looks much older. I can see the black paint is coming off especially on the side car. It could do with a fresh coat. Perhaps your Father could paint it for you." And the Officer handed back the model to Art.

"He can't," said Art, "He's driving a tank but it's a secret where he is."

"Oh I have heard of these landships, as they are called. We should be seeing more of them on the battlefields, especially on the front lines. They are a very new weapon. Your Father must be a very important soldier to be allowed to drive one."

Stan and Alice listened to the man with interest and began to wonder just what battlefields he was referring to. The man smiled at the children and said, "Did you see anyone walking on this path as you came along. I am waiting to meet my young lady here. She's quite late and I don't have much home leave at present before I have to go back."

At that the man looked pale and a little shaky. He put his hands over his ears as if to protect them against noise. Then he added, "It's so peaceful here. I often dream of this place when the guns start up and the shelling. This is my favourite tree. My sister and I used to climb it as children, before I was sent away to school and Military training. We had some strange adventures in this tree, I can tell you." The Officer leant his back against the tree and sighed. "There are no trees left anymore near the trenches."

Stanley looked at the sad face of the Officer and said, "It's our favourite tree too; as you say it's a very special place, especially for adventures."

"We met Charlie Chaplin up the tree and a bloke called Jack," said Art, glad to get the man's attention away from his precious toy motorbike.

"You never know whom you are going to meet in this Forest," said the Officer. "Sometimes the one you really want to meet just doesn't turn up. I've come here so often to find her. I can't understand why she doesn't come. It's so hard back on the Somme, with the shells, and the gunfire and now the gas." At this moment, the Officer seemed to become quite agitated and he stepped away from the tree to peer again down the path towards the cottage.

"Oh Molly where are you? I have been waiting so long." The man spoke to himself and then returned to lean against the comfort of the old tree trunk. He turned towards the children. "We used to meet here before the war started, my sweetheart and me. We're getting married in the village Church when this wretched war is over. I need to tell her that so she can get everything ready. Are you sure you didn't see her walking passed the little cottage, near this path? "

Alice touched the man's arm and looked more closely at his face. She gasped a little as she remembered the photograph of the young World War 1 Captain which Auntie Molly had on the dresser in her house. Was this man Auntie Molly's sweetheart and Auntie Nellie's brother? If so, why had he come and what was it he wanted Alice wondered.

"Sorry Sir, Alice said gently to the Officer, "We haven't seen anyone coming onto the path just now. Could you tell us your name in case we meet up with the lady you mentioned?"

"Of course; I am so sorry children, not to have properly introduced myself. I 'm Captain Frank Winter, serving in the Royal Engineers, currently in charge of communications and dispatches on the Somme. We've great motorbikes, son, just like yours". The Captain seemed to have recovered some calm and managed to wink and smile at Art as well as saluting Stan and Alice.

Alice introduced herself and Stan to the Captain and he shook hands with them both.

The Officer spoke quietly, looking away from Art who was playing in the leaves with Rabbit and the motorbike.

"It's bad there now at the Somme. We've lost so many, hundreds, to German guns across the trenches. Men like your father, Stan are so brave. They ride their motor bikes across the trenches to get messages to Command and some carry the wounded in their side cars back to the Field hospitals. I hope he is safe and comes home to you soon."

Stan did not argue with this courageous man but wondered what his Dad would think about carrying a wounded soldier in his sidecar. Stan wondered where his Dad was now but knew for certain that he was not in the battle lines of the Somme which, he had learned from his History books, had happened more than twenty years earlier in the First World War. Stan felt relief but was deeply puzzled as to how this serving Officer could be here in the Forest, away from the fighting at the Somme. How strange time is Stanley thought to himself, but he knew that somehow he was meant to help this Captain Winter. Stanley had no doubt that this was the man who had crafted the model motorbike and side car for Molly which was now Art's pride and joy.

Captain Winter leaned harder into the Tree and lifted one leg behind him pressing his booted foot against the bark. He turned to Alice and said,

"I wonder if she hasn't got my letters. Perhaps she didn't know I would be here, waiting for her. Logistics are so difficult at the moment. Or perhaps she's forgotten me and found a new sweetheart."

Alice looked startled and said quickly, "Oh no; she has never forgotten you; she has your photograph on the dresser. I know she speaks to it every night."

"You do know her, I thought you might. How is she? Where is she? Is she coming to meet me?"

At this the Officer became more agitated and moved away from the tree to hold Alice's arms and to look her fully in the face. Alice realised that she had said too much and this was causing him to become quite distressed. Stanley interrupted and Captain Frank turned towards him, letting go of Alice's arms.

"I think we do know the lady you mean, Sir; perhaps, as you say, she hasn't received your letters. We know she cares about you and your sister. I think they are friends."

"My Molly and my Nell; such good friends. How I miss them. I've been away too long. Perhaps you could make sure that Molly gets this letter."

Captain Frank reached into the top pocket of his jacket and withdrew a folded paper which he handed to Stanley.

Stanley saw that the letter was splattered with dark stains, the brownish red of old blood. He managed not to show his shock and placed it carefully in his pocket.

"I will Sir," he said, "I am sure you will meet again one day."

"Thank you, son," said Captain Frank, who now sounded weary, "I must go. My men are waiting for me. So many brave young men lost, such a waste of young life. Goodbye, dear children. Take care of my Sunbeam, Art who is 7 years old. Just the right person to guard it!"

Captain Frank Winter turned his back on the children and walked from under the tree and onto the path, appearing to gradually dissolve in the distance. Alice and Stanley stared after him and both gasped as they noted the large wound in the back of his head and neck, just under the military cap, as well as the badly blood stained back of his uniform jacket. Alice let out a little cry and put her hand to her mouth; Stan felt shaken but took Alice's hand and said,

"It was what the Tree wanted, Alice, we were needed to help Captain Winter find some peace. He and Molly had unfinished things in their lives. He needed to know that Molly had his letter and that he planned to come home to get married."

Alice looked pale and tearful but said,

"You are right, Stanley, perhaps Molly needed to know that as well."

It was lucky that Art was busy playing with his motorbike and loading the sidecar with leaves and so he did not see the wound in Captain Frank's head and the blood stains on his smart uniform.

Stan took the faded, stained letter from his pocket and began to unfold it. Alice stopped him for a moment and said,

"I am not sure we should read it, Stan. It's a private love letter, I think."

"Yes, you're right Alice but I think we should check there is nothing in it to hurt Auntie Molly."

Both children looked at the faded pencil handwriting which read,

Dearest Sweetheart, Mollie, I am missing you every moment of every day. I cannot wait to be home again, to walk in our Forest with you. I dream every night of meeting you again under our Tree and of our wedding in the old Church when I am next on leave. Until then remember me and our love always. Your Frank, the Somme October 1916.

Alice and Stanley agreed that this was a most important letter but they were unsure how to get it into Molly's hands without alarming her.

"We must think of something," Stanley said, feeling short of any ideas at all.

Then Art jumped up from his game, "Look at this Stan, there's a big space in the sidecar and Rabbit just about fits his legs in it."

"Not only Rabbit," said Stan to Alice. "Perhaps we may have found a way."

Both children noticed that the wind in the trees had calmed and that the leaves of the old Oak above their heads were rustling a sound like a gentle thank you.

"I think we are free to go," said Alice to Stanley and with that the children started along the path to Auntie Nell's cottage.

CHAPTER 13: MOTOR BIKE MAIL

Auntie Nell was pleased to see the three children return safely from their walk in time for tea but she frowned and felt some concern at the serious faces that Stanley and Alice presented. In contrast Art played at giving rides to Rabbit in the toy motor bike and appeared happy and excited.

Freddy arrived, pink cheeked and full of his game of football in which he had scored two goals. He gave Alice and Stan a very lively account with a full demonstration of how he had kicked the ball to score. The leg and arm movements put Auntie Nell's vase at risk as he knocked the little table on which it sat, dusty but safe. Luckily Stan caught the ornament as it toppled.

"Careful Freddy," he said "You're not on the football field now."

"It was a great game,"said Freddy, calming down a bit. "What's wrong with you two? Why so gloomy."

"We're not gloomy, just thoughtful. Trying to sort out a problem." said Alice.

"Oh no, not that Tree again!!" said Freddy collapsing into the nearby armchair. "You've been climbing today, haven't you? What's the challenge now? I will help."

"Not exactly climbing, Freddy. We think we met Captain Winter just under the Tree's large branches, leaning against the trunk. He was waiting for Auntie Molly!" said Stan quietly.

Freddy looked shocked and rested his chin on his football. He was aware of the photograph of the handsome young soldier which Molly Brown kept in pride of place on her dresser. He listened in surprise to Alice and Stan as they described to him their meeting with the Captain, how he had recognised the model motorbike and side car which Art was playing with, and how he appeared to be waiting for his sweetheart in their special meeting place. Freddy gasped as Stan carefully took the stained piece of paper from his pocket and said,

"We promised Captain Frank that we would get this to Molly; just not sure how to do it. We can't just give it to her".

"Why not?" said Freddy, "I'll do it."

"Oh Freddy, think about it." said Alice softly, " We can't just say we bumped into a man who turned out to be a ghost or a memory or something we just don't understand."

Freddy did think about it and nodded and sighed, just as Art wheeled the toy motorbike into the room and sat on the floor still playing with it. The three older children looked at the motor bike, all with the same idea. Freddy asked Art to come into the garden and play football so that he could show Art how brilliant he was at scoring goals. Art was flattered to be asked and gave his beloved motor bike and Rabbit to Stan for safe keeping.

When Freddy and Art were in the garden, Alice took the old love letter from Stan and folded it very carefully before pushing it into the hollow end of the side car where there had been space for Rabbit's paws.

A few minutes later Nellie and Molly asked the children to come round the kitchen table for some tea. There was new bread which Nellie had baked and some of her plum jam which she had bottled from the previous year's harvest. Molly unwrapped some brown paper and showed everyone the small piece of cheese she had managed to buy in town despite the food shortages and rationing. Gwen crept under the table by the children, hoping for crumbs.

As the adults and children ate, Freddy told everyone for the tenth time about his goal scoring skills. Rabbit sat at the end of the table, next to Art with his feet pushed into the side car of the wooden model bike. His body flopped forward and Art managed to get jam on the best yellow waistcoat as he tried to sit him up.

Auntie Nell laughed and said, "Artie, give Rabbit to me and I will wipe the jam from his new waistcoat. We can't have him all sticky."

As she spoke, Nell leaned across the table and pulled Rabbit out of the side car with quite a tug. As his legs flew up in the air, a small folded piece of paper fell from them and fluttered to the floor where Molly was sitting. Freddy, Alice and Stanley gasped, then held their breath as Molly bent to pick up the paper and began to unfold it.

"Whatsoever is that Molly?" asked Nell, "Must've been stuck in there years by the looks of it."

Molly looked pale as she read the note and was unable to speak for a few moments. She then put the paper to her lips and kissed the name at the bottom of the note. After a minute of silence which seemed like hours to the children, Molly took a deep breath and said,

"It's from our boy, it's from Frank, Nellie. Perhaps he left it for me to find when he was last on leave or perhaps it came with that telegram and I couldn't look at it all those years ago. I don't know. I just know I am so glad to have it now."

Molly passed the note across the table for Nell to look at. Nell noticed the faded brownish-red stains but said nothing about these.

"He was coming home to marry you, Molly, just like he said he would. Thank you Art and Rabbit for finding this treasure," and Nell passed the letter back to Molly who placed it safely in a handkerchief in her bag.

Art had no idea what was happening but knew that Auntie Nell and Molly were somehow pleased that Rabbit had sat in the side car of his motor bike. So after the jam was cleaned off his waistcoat, Rabbit resumed his pride of place on the motorbike.

After tea, Stan, Alice and Freddy were allowed to return to the sitting room, supposedly to discuss their return to school. They sat on the floor and Alice began to smile, "I can't believe it. It worked and Molly made her own reasons for not having the note all those years ago." she whispered.

"I am not sure that Auntie Nell believed it," said Stan, " She looked so carefully at the blood stains. Still we did what the Tree wanted. Perhaps now Captain Frank might have peace and not have to keep coming to their Tree to find his sweetheart; oh and Molly knows that the wedding was definitely happening."

Freddy snorted, "What a lot of rot. Who wants to get married when you can play football!" and with that Freddy jumped up and challenged the other two to a game in the garden.

Art joined the fun outside and left his motor bike and Rabbit on the kitchen table. Nell picked up the model and looked at it thoughtfully. She unhooked the side car and placed her fingers into the well of the front, where she pulled out some damp leaves.

"Maybe the leaves stained that note," she thought to herself, " although the marks looked like old bloodstains to me." She placed the toy back on the table and picked up Rabbit to inspect him for jammy fingers.

"Well, Mr Rabbit, you and your friends have had some adventures here in our Forest and done some good too in these scary times, I am sure. Molly waited twenty four years for that letter and it was delivered today by a toy motor bike. How very odd is that!"

Molly had been standing by the sitting room window watching the children playing and laughing in the late autumn sunshine. She turned to Nelly and said quietly,

"How strange that today of all days the letter should be found. It is the anniversary of Frank's death on the Somme. It's as if he knew we needed to see it. It's odd I never found it in his little model motorbike before now. I think these children are a blessing sent to us, Nell."

"Children always are, my friend, at least that's what my old mother and her mother before her used to say. What was it now? Oh yes, 'suffer the little children to come unto me.' Well these London children came unto us, Molly and we are the better for it." Nellie tapped Rabbit's head as she spoke.

With that the ladies began to gather the plates to wash up, only to find that Gwen had sneaked to the table during all the commotion and had given the plates a good wash with her tongue.

Rabbit was hoping that Gwen would not give him as well a good lick clean, especially as he was now the proud owner of a new title.

"**Mr** Rabbit, indeed," he said to himself, "**Mr** Rabbit indeed I am." And he looked and felt less floppy.

Auntie Molly, Alice and Freddy left the little cottage and drove to Molly's house. There Alice noticed Molly place Frank's letter in the frame of the photograph as she whispered,

"Goodnight, my darling; see you in my dreams."

Alice hoped she would, just as she hoped to see her mother and father in her own dreams.

Back at the cottage, Stan, Art, Mr Rabbit and the motor bike were soon tucked up in the two beds with Gwen sleeping between them.

"What was it that Rabbit found in the sidecar, Stan?" asked Art sleepily, thinking about the odd teatime they had just had. "Did it belong to the soldier we met in the Forest? I wonder if we will see him again; he might know our Dad."

"We won't see him again, Art and I don't think he knows our Dad, but you and Rabbit did a good thing today, finding that note amongst the leaves. It belonged to Molly." But Art was already asleep and dreaming of his father and the real motorbike.

Nelly sat downstairs dozing in front of the fire. She became aware of the Forest wind whipping fiercely around the cottage door and she spoke to it,

"Enough of your adventures and mysteries for now, Trees, we all need some rest."

And with that the cottage and the forest settled down for a peaceful night.

CHAPTER 14: POST WAR

That is the end of our story. The magic, mystery, love and courage of our tale is everywhere, not just in Forests. And Children, you may wonder about the fate of the noble and magnificent ancient Oak Tree. I believe it is still there in the dark, mysterious part of the Forest. If you listen carefully you may hear it call to you.

You will want to know what happened to our brave children. Stan and Art stayed for another year with Auntie Nell in the cottage. Then they went to live with their Mother, Aunt and Uncle on the farm in Kent. They went for holidays with Auntie Nell who became one of the family. Dad came back at the end of the War when he worked on the farm introducing and managing the new tractors and motor vehicles which were coming in. The beloved motorbike and side car were stored in a barn and rarely used as the family bought a Ford Motor car. Art grew up to be a skilled mechanic who restored old cars and bikes. He never let go of his model Sunbeam motor bike which was in pride of place on his workbench. He had hazy memories of his childhood adventures in the Forest but remained convinced that he had once met Charlie Chaplin.

Stan became a top student, the first in his family to go to university, where he studied history and archaeology.

He became a Professor and made discoveries of ancient objects on archaeological digs. He talked to his students about the mystery of time and the treasured memories the Earth holds for us all if we can just pay attention to what it is asking. As a young man he visited Auntie Nell and discussed with her some of the childhood adventures he had with the others in the Forest. She was now an older lady but she patted his hand and said there were always adventures to find and that she knew the Tree which he described.

Alice became a scientist and studied plants, trees and insects. She spent many years telling the world of the importance of nature and how it must be protected at all costs. She was especially interested in how trees communicate with each other and how they released chemical messages to inform each other about dangers. Alice's parents also returned from the War after completing intelligence work in somewhere called Bletchley Park. They never told Alice exactly what they had done but always said that a mystery could be solved by applying Science.

Freddy of course became a professional footballer and played for a few years with a famous team. Later he opened a small hotel near the Forest and spent regular visits with Nellie and Molly. The four children stayed in touch over the years and remained firm friends.

And Rabbit?? As he grew older he received many knitted replacement parts for his anatomy, and regular new waistcoats. He became the much loved property of Art's own little boy, Roddy.

"Roddy and Rabbit. Now that seems just right." Art had said to his old friend.

Rabbit had looked Art straight in the eyes and seemed to reply,

"**Mr** Rabbit, Mate, if you don't mind".

The end

SOME HISTORY NOTES

CHAPTER 1 AND 2: World War 2 (1939-1945) started when Germany under the Nazi Party invaded other European countries. Britain, France America and Russia fought against them. Other countries, all over the World became involved. Early in the War London and other British Cities were heavily bombed in air raids. Many people were killed. The Government evacuated lots of children into homes in the country side to keep them safe.

CHAPTER 4: King Charles 1 ruled Britain in the 1600's. He argued with Parliament because he believed that God had given him the right to rule over everyone and not have to answer to the elected men of Parliament. Oliver Cromwell led Parliament into a Civil War in England. His army were called The Roundheads because of the shape of their helmets. The King's side were called The Royalists and Cavaliers. After many battles Cromwell won. King Charles 1 was executed in London in front of crowds in 1649. His son escaped to France. After many years and failed attempts to raise an Army, Charles was asked to come back to England and was crowned King Charles 11 in 1660. He took revenge on those that had beheaded his father.

CHAPTER 5 AND 6: Jack Shepherd also known as Gentleman Jack and Honest Jack(1702-1724) Jack was born in the East End of London to a poor family. After his father died his mother could not feed him and he was placed in the workhouse aged 6 years. Eventually he was apprenticed to a carpenter but after a while became a thief and highwayman. He was caught and imprisoned several times but always managed to escape through cleverness and strength. He became a celebrity of his day with rich and famous people paying to visit him in prison. He was caught and hanged in 1724.

CHAPTER 8, 9 AND 10: Children from poor families and those kept in the Parish Workhouses because they had no families who could look after them, were apprenticed to learn trades. One of these was very cruel. Small boys were apprenticed to Chimney Sweeps who taught them to climb the maze of chimneys in the houses of the day. This would loosen the soot from the coal and wood fires which burnt in the grates. (No Central heating then.) They had horrible living conditions and nasty accidents and death often resulted. Several attempts were made to end this cruelty. Finally in 1875 Parliament passed an Act to put a stop to this trade in Children.

CHAPTER 11: Food was in short supply during WW2 because it was difficult to import safely and many farm workers had to join the armed forces. Women were recruited to work on the farms. People were given ration books with coupons entitling them to a small amount of different food stuffs like meat and cheese. Imagine this now with all the fast food joints closed down. How would you manage??

CHAPTER 12 AND 13: World War 1 (1914-1918) Great Britain and its Allies, Russia and France fought the Germans and Austrians. This was a terrible war killing 8.5 million soldiers and many civilians. Many very young men died, leaving orphans and widows. It was fought in trenches in France as well as at sea. With the help of the USA Britain and her Allies won. However the aftermath was thought to be one of the causes of World War 2.

.

Printed in Great Britain
by Amazon

86303415R00071